CW00514964

AUTHOR'S NOTE

In 2020 scientists began growing meat developed from human cells in labs. It is called the ouroboros steak.

CHAPTER 1

He stopped, just like he had learned so many years ago. His foot hit the ground and then froze, his entire body tensing behind it to stop the motion. Not enough tension that it would impede his ability to explode with threat and fury on a split second's notice, but sufficient to keep him from being seen.

Cotton Wiley's eyes continued to move through the Ruggedized Night Vision Goggles, observing the forty degrees of green landscape ahead of him that the technology afforded.

He heard breathing behind him—slow and labored. The two of them had been moving fast down the Texas Thirty-Five frontage road for nearly an hour and it was easy for him to forget that she was only twelve. She was already five eight and she was tough, just like her daddy. Never in a million years would she ask him to slow down. Jean Wiley would keep grinding it out without pause, just like her father always had. Just like he had taught her, even if he hadn't meant to.

Cotton reached down and tugged on the rope that was latched to the carabiner on his belt. Three sharp tugs. That was the code to hold fast. He knew she was nearly blind in the darkness and verbal communication would give away their position, so this method was the only way.

The lights had gone out several months before, so now this was how they traveled. Cotton knew it was scary for her to just keep plunging forward into the darkness, in a tunnel to hell that seemed to have no end. Maybe it was better that way as she couldn't see hell's monsters, even if they were everywhere around her.

Cotton held his gaze on the string of cars that stretched out over Interstate Thirty-Five, the length of road just parallel to where they now stood. Then he saw it again. It was movement. He brought his short barrel rifle up, not to fire it but to trigger the infrared illuminator. The Steiner DBAL cast its beam across the road, lighting up everything in his path. This briefly made Cotton think about the bag of batteries in his rucksack. How many remained? Was it seventeen or eighteen? Cotton still had to power the DBAL and his night optic device. He knew he had about twenty hours of night vision on a single CR123 battery. At some point, he was going to run out of light.

Jean couldn't see any of this. The infrared light cast by the DBAL laser illuminator was invisible, unless you were looking through night vision like the RNVG's mounted to Cotton's bump helmet. He'd discarded his high cut ballistic helmet long ago. It had been a hard decision to make, but in the end, it made sense. He just wasn't getting in those kinds of fire fights that he needed a lot of armor. Most of the people he ran into, he was just cutting through like a hot knife through butter. Plus, as much as he would like to have believed he was still the same man who had filled his boots twenty years prior, he just wasn't. While the bump helmet offered no protection against gunfire, it was a hell of a lot lighter than its ballistic counterpart.

He was a little older, a lot slower and had never fully recovered from all the concussions and TBIs he had suffered in Iraq and Afghanistan. Hell, everything was hard. Not just getting in fights or moving through the night. Opening a can of SPAM seemed weirdly challenging. He would find himself standing slumped over and staring off into the darkness, and Jean would need to snap him out of it. Then he felt like he wanted to cry. He never did, but he knew she could sense it. She could sense that something was wrong with her father. So, she would give him a hug and tell him he was the best daddy in the world.

There was movement again, and this time Cotton could clearly see what he was looking at. It was the figure of a man, and in that man's hand was a rifle. Then there was another man, and another, and another. There were six of them. The moon was shining just enough that none of them were using flashlights. That moonlight offered enough illumination that they could see their way forward, but they wouldn't be able to see far into the distance.

Shit, Cotton thought to himself as he saw the lone figure that these men were clearly pursuing.

It was either a woman or a small man. There was still a reasonable amount of distance between the small figure and the pursuers. Maybe enough that he or she could get away?

No. They were quickly closing the gap. Then he understood why. The figure they were pursuing looked like his or her hands were bound.

Not your business, Cotton thought to himself.

Then his thought process shifted. What if it was a woman? What if it was a young woman? What if it was Jean? Wouldn't he want someone to step in if his daughter was in a situation like this? Like his wife had been.

Texas was lawless, and everyone knew it. That was why he had chosen to travel through what was now called the Texas Meat Belt. Less chance of government interference. What remained of the Federal Police didn't have the balls to step foot into central Texas, which gave him and his daughter free passage to get where they were going.

This also meant that it was open season on anyone caught out there, including this woman. It was a woman; he knew it. The whole game of "it could be a man or a woman" had been bullshit. No, it was a woman, and she was in trouble. Men with guns didn't pursue a woman in this part of the country with anything other than ill intentions.

Cotton turned and scanned his surroundings. He saw it. It was perfect. The perfect height and the perfect size.

Cotton tugged on the rope again and led Jean to the tree, where he unhooked her from his carabiner and moved her toward it.

"It's a woman," he whispered. "She's in trouble."

"Like Mom?" Jean asked.

Cotton's blood ran cold, and he felt a knot in his throat.

"Yeah," he answered. "Like Mom."

Jean nodded her understanding. She reached into her fanny pack and retrieved the little Springfield Hellcat pistol that she carried. It wasn't her father's first choice for a gun or even his second or third, but it fit well in her small hand and she seemed able to manage the muzzle flip.

The plan was always the same. When it was time for Daddy to do business, that meant it was time for little Jean to get up a tree, and she could climb a tree just like she was ringing a bell. Cotton watched her scamper up the side of the old oak before finally settling onto a large limb. She knew the drill. Daddy would always come back to get her. If someone else came, she would hit the white light attached to the pistol to blind them and then send them to hell. Even if there were more of them with better armament, she would still have a fighting chance shooting down from an elevated position.

Cotton began moving to the interstate. He did a brass check and felt the 5.56 round in the chamber of his Daniel Defense M4. The rifle had been with him through a lot, both overseas and ever since the collapse. It had never failed and it wouldn't now. He knew it.

As he moved off the frontage road and across the grassy divide to the six-lane freeway, he could feel the wet ground beneath him, but it wasn't wet from the rain. It was the humidity. It had been humid back in Virginia, but not like this.

"She's in that one!" He heard a voice call out in the darkness.

Cotton watched through his NODs (night optic device) and he was close enough to make out facial features. Maybe only one hundred yards away from them. Close enough to decide which eye he wanted to shoot out.

It was also close enough for them to hear him, even if they couldn't see him. This wasn't the time to get cocky. He understood better than most that you never know who you're dealing with. It would be just his luck to roll up on an organized force of pipe hitting former Army Rangers. That would be a bad day for all concerned.

Even if that were the case, he would still come out on top. He knew it. He knew this because it had to be that way. It had to be because Jean needed her daddy to come back and get her out of that tree.

Cotton froze for a moment and felt it welling up

in his gut again. It was that feeling. The feeling that there should be some way for him to make things normal again, to set things right. To give his daughter her future back.

He tightened his hand on the pistol grip of the M4 and looked down at the blurry outline of the weapon. He looked at the rifle in his hands and received the answer to his question of how to set things right. How to give his daughter her future back. This was the way. There was no other. At least not any he knew of.

Cotton looked back to the distance one hundred yards away and saw the men moving between the cars. He held his position and counted the opposition force. There were six of them. They were wearing what looked to be some kind of mix and match military uniforms. Probably just civilians who had bought a bunch of stuff on Amazon before everything fell apart.

Two of them had rifles, and the rest looked like they were only carrying handguns.

He moved forward, feet gliding across the ground, one beside the other. Less hip sway in a tight stance meant less wobble when he started putting his laser on targets. Should he wait? Wait for some kind of positive identification before he started sending these men to their heavenly reward?

No. Not out here. Not in the Texas Meat Belt, that was for damn sure.

Cotton hit the button to activate his aiming laser and put it on the head of the last man in the stack that was moving down the interstate. Now he was only fifty yards away. Impossible to miss at that range. Just like the illuminator, he could see the IR laser, but they could not.

He pressed the trigger on his M4. Not a pull, but a press. It was like drawing a line in the sand with your fingertip. That was where people screwed up. They slapped that trigger like a red-headed stepchild instead of gently pressing it in the direction they want it to go.

Cotton watched the first man go down. The dead man crumpled to the ground on the interstate. There was no drama to it, no final glory. Just a soul exiting a body and that body returning to the earth in the least ceremonious way possible.

No one had noticed it yet. One man jerked his head to the right, probably after he heard something, but did not notice the last man in the stack going down. Before he had time to investigate further, Cotton executed him. Then the next man.

"Contact right!" A voice shouted.

The man calling the alarm sounded scared. Cotton caught onto this. These men weren't warriors, they were just bullies.

He let some of his caution go and moved faster up the embankment to the concrete. As he crested it, he came face to face with one man who must have run to the guard rail while Cotton was coming up the other side. The perfect timing for a real bad time.

It was reflex. Reflex built from hundreds of direct action raids in close quarters in Iraq. Cotton slammed the rifle forward, suppressor checking the man in the throat. No sooner had the suppressor slammed into the man's Adam's apple than Cotton pressed his trigger, opening up the would-be attacker's throat to the night and severing his spinal cord.

There was no hesitation as Cotton stepped over the guard rail, but then he did pause for a split second on the top of that rail, one foot in contact and one foot hanging into the night as he again pressed his trigger. In that moment of stepping over the rail, he had seen another target present itself, and this man also crumpled to the ground a split second after Cotton put his infrared laser on the target's chest.

Now there was only one pursuer left. Cotton watched him scramble between the abandoned cars, his head snapping wildly from left to right. This man was now only twenty meters away. Whoever he was, he still hadn't activated a white light. This was smart, as the only thing a flashlight would have done in this situation was give Cotton the clearest target possible to unload on.

Cotton walked onto the interstate with his rifle at the low ready. For all intents and purposes, he was invisible in the darkness. He stopped just ten meters from the man. Then he saw it. Movement out of the corner of his eye coming from one of the abandoned cars. He started to bring his weapon up when he realized what it was. Who it was.

It was the woman these men had been chasing. She had crawled into the back of a minivan and was hiding.

"Who are you?" The man shouted. "A Kingsman? We're treaty members!"

That figured, Cotton thought to himself. Treaty members weren't organized enough to be Kingsmen, and they also weren't civil enough to be in one of the cities.

"Ain't no Kingsman," Cotton said. "I know how to read and write."

The man raised his gun and Cotton responded

by activating his visible laser and putting it on the man's chest.

The man looked down and saw the glowing red dot on his shirt. His pistol dropped to the ground with a clatter.

"Who are you?" He asked. "Really?"

Cotton switched his laser back to IR, rendering it invisible to the naked eye. He was close enough to see the man's eyes. Even though he couldn't see color through the night vision device, he could see the pale, milky gloss over the man's pupils.

"A free thinker," Cotton said. "Looks like you went the other way."

"Oh, I see," the man spat. "Like you knew what was gonna happen if you took it."

"Didn't know one way or the other," Cotton said. "And ain't no use crying over it now."

There was a palpable shift in the air, the tension between the two men that had been tight as a trip wire now sagged. There was no question what the outcome of this exchange would be.

"I didn't ask for this," the man said, his voice quieter.

"I know," Cotton replied with a hint of sympathy.

"I'm just trying to make it out here."

Cotton put his laser in the kill box between the man's eyes. The splash from the IR light further illuminated the pale quality of those eyes.

"We all are."

It was quiet again. It had been quiet before, but not like this. Now there was no more of the sound of men or their machines in the world. Despite everything that had happened, the hard fighting, the suffering and the seemingly unending wave of death, Cotton did appreciate that one thing: That silence.

No more sounds of civilization. No more dinging phones, no car engines, no voices in the background, no nothing. All that was left of it was the void they all now lived in. He knew it wasn't like that in the cities. If anything, it was far worse than it had ever been before because of how the Consumers had packed themselves into those places like rats.

Not out here, though. In places like central Texas, it was just the void, the quiet. At night, it was even better. Perhaps that was because Cotton was so accustomed to working at night. That was the way it had always been. Sleep all day, then wake up, turn on some Slayer and workout. Once the sun set it was time to hunt.

Cotton walked quietly down the road and saw the minivan ahead of him. She wasn't moving, but she was still inside of it. He scanned his surroundings again and saw no one there. It was a calculated risk, but one he had to take.

He reached down and adjusted the bezel on the Surefire light mounted to his rifle from infrared to white light, then pressed the tail cap button and released it to leave the light on, pointing it to the ground. As he did this, he flipped up his nods. It took a moment for his eyes to adjust to the light. He sure as hell hoped there wasn't some sniper out there waiting for him to do something stupid like this. If there was, he probably wouldn't know about it until some angel told him.

"It's okay," he whispered. "I'm not one of them."

Even as he said this, he kept his thumb on the selector switch of his M4. If things went south, he would be at a hell of a disadvantage, but he'd been there before. It was nothing new.

Shit, he thought to himself. *This is a bad idea.*

Cotton moved toward the minivan, bringing the Surefire up to light his way. It was bright as hell, so he had to be careful not to shine it in this woman's eyes and blind her. The sliding door was halfway open, so he stopped.

"I need you to come out," he said sternly. "I can't help you if you don't, but I'm not opening that door. You have to come to me."

For a moment, nothing happened. Then he saw two shaking hands emerge from the door. They were bound with what looked like bailing wire. One hand gripped the sliding door and pulled it open. The screeching of the long dry track wheel seemed to scream through the night as the door slowly rolled open.

She sat on the floor of the minivan and looked up at Cotton.

Cotton clipped off the bailing wire with his multitool and then handed her a small bottle of water that had been in his cargo pocket.

She was pretty enough in a hard Texas way, but the last couple of years had clearly taken a toll on her, just like they had on everyone. He figured she was biologically in her late twenties, but she looked like a hard thirty-five at best.

"I..." she started and then stopped. Her tongue protruded slowly and she licked her lips then continued. "My name is April."

"Pleased to meet you April. I'm Cotton."

"What kind of name is Cotton?" She asked.

"Family name," he replied. He scanned the road again and then looked back to her. "But I don't think this is the time or the place to be having our first heart to heart."

The two of them walked back through the darkness. This time it was April holding the rope that was attached to Cotton's belt as he navigated the black void through his night vision. In the distance ahead, he could see the tree that Jean had gone up, and he stopped.

He put his fingers to his lips and whistled once. That was the signal for his daughter to make her way down to meet him.

Cotton continued his forward movement, his head always turning subtly from side to side. There was no peripheral vision through the RNVG's, because it was effectively like looking through two toilet paper tubes. A man had to develop the habit of continually scanning by turning his head from side to side as he wore them.

Finally, they reached the base of the tree and stopped. Cotton whistled again and this time another whistle responded about twenty feet away from where the trunk of the tree lay.

"Okay," Cotton said quietly. "We're good."

They made no introductions. There was no back and forth. April and Jean walked through the darkness behind their protector, each one holding a rope that connected them to him. Cotton navigated carefully down a steep slope and into a small ravine. It wasn't very deep, but it was enough to give them some cover for the night.

He dropped his pack and instantly felt as if someone had lifted the weight of the world from his shoulders. Cotton Wiley had always been strong. That wasn't the problem. The problem was that with age, the strength remained and became enough to hammer his joints until their screaming was the only thing he heard. Not that it mattered much, because no matter how weak his joints became or how strong his muscles remained, his mind was the strongest, and it would never quit.

Cotton reached into the pack and retrieved a small bag from it. Within the bag were rolls of fishing line, stakes and camp alarms. The kind that would set off an ear-splitting siren if the line was broken.

"Just wait here," Cotton said, more for April than for Jean. His daughter knew the drill by now. "I'll be back soon."

Light was a commodity. At least, in the darkness, it was. It was a precious commodity, and it was expensive. Just a little light was enough to bring a world of darkness down on your head if you mis-used it. This meant that Cotton was very careful about where he allowed the light to get in. Some nights they just stayed in the darkness, but it was easy to lose yourself that way. It was easier for your sanity to slip away in that endless black.

It was more his daughter that he worried about than himself. He knew his days were numbered, at least when it came to his brain working. While his mind wouldn't quit, his actual physical brain was failing. He knew it. He could feel it every day, and he worried that Jean saw it as well.

Alone in the darkness again, he moved in a box formation around their campsite, putting the stakes in the ground and running the wire between them with the alarms attached.

For a moment, he wondered if he should have left his daughter alone with a complete stranger. If this had all been some elaborate ruse to get to her, it was a hell of a play. Even if it was, the would-be kidnappers would get a lot more than they bargained for. Jean wasn't some pushover. She wasn't a normal twelve-year-old. At least, not how they used to be.

Cotton's mind flashed back to that car on the road in Arkansas. It was a screwup. It was a screw up of epic proportions. He had left her hiding in a car on the road with her Hellcat while he scouted ahead. Logically, he knew it wasn't his fault, but emotionally, he could never forgive himself for how it all went down.

Back then, they still had walkies, and he had been a half mile down the highway when hers started triggering. Over and over, but no voice. Just the call button getting hit repeatedly, like she was fumbling for it. Somehow, he knew that was what was happening.

He'd never run so fast. Not in all of his life. His feet hammered the unforgiving Arkansas pavement, while the heat seared his lungs and his eyes blurred. Yet all the motor mechanics he had been practicing for his entire adult life came into play as he closed in on the car she had been hiding in.

He brought his M4 up and sighted the EOTech

reticle on the back of the head he saw. It was a man's head. He was on top of her.

God. No. Please God, no.

Then the first shot broke. And then another. And another. And another but they weren't his.

Cotton pulled the car door open and grabbed the man by his shirt collar. He yanked him out of the vehicle, what was left of his head coming apart as he threw him to the ground.

Jean's Hellcat came up and sighted in on him. Cotton dropped his rifle from his left hand and held both hands up.

"No baby! It's me! It's daddy!"

Jean's eyes were wild. Her small finger was on the trigger, tensed for a moment, and then it relaxed. Her face was covered in blood and brain matter. Cotton took the gun from her and scooped her up in his arms. Then he felt it, the spasming of her body. He knew what was happening. It was her first kill.

He set her down on the pavement and held her hair back as she threw up.

It hadn't been like that for him. People always said you would throw up or feel some kind of crushing guilt the first time you took a life, but that wasn't the truth. In fact, it hadn't been that way for any of the guys in the Teams. The first time he had sighted in and killed a man in Afghanistan, he felt nothing. It was just a job. A thing that happened. There were different theories about this. Maybe it was constant exposure to violence in the media, or that video games that trivialized the taking of human life had trained them.

This was different. He had been a twenty-two year old Navy SEAL. She was a twelve-year-old girl.

Cotton checked his daughter and found that she was still physically intact. She had not been harmed. Whatever that man had been trying to do, Jean Wiley had ended him before he had a chance to do it. Her attacker thought he had found a victim. Instead, he found a warrior.

The man wouldn't be the last one she would send to hell that year.

Cotton walked back to the make-shift campground. After performing his reconnaissance of the area, he knew they were alone. At least, as far as he could tell. There was always the possibility that someone else was out there. If that was the case, whoever that someone was, he was better at this than Cotton. There weren't a lot of those men walking the earth, but Cotton knew they existed. He had met them but hoped he wouldn't be meeting them again anytime soon.

When he was younger, that would have been a different story. He would have craved the challenge, would have wanted to prove he was the biggest swinging dick in the valley. Back then, if it was proven that he wasn't, it would have only meant him meeting his end. Now the narrative had shifted. He couldn't take stupid risks just to prove a point. Failure wouldn't only mean him stepping into the darkness forever, it would mean his little girl being left alone.

Cotton stopped at the inner perimeter he had established and whistled. Another whistle answered his call and he walked another two dozen feet. As usual, he could see them, but they could not see him. He reached forward and turned the dial that shut off his RNVG's, then hit the button that unlocked his Wilcox mount from the forward position and raised them up on his helmet. He could feel the relief in his eyes. Looking through that green phosphor screen for hours on end wasn't easy. The older he got, the more of a toll it took on his eyes.

He dropped to a knee and rooted around in his small ruck sack until he found the solar lantern. It had a red filter that shined a shallow amber light as he popped it open. He saw panic in April's eyes. Jean saw it too and put her hand on the woman's shoulder.

"It's okay," Jean said. "Daddy did his recon. We're alone. Right?" She asked, looking at her father.

Cotton nodded and sat down on a rock.

"Near as I can tell," Cotton said. "And that light won't travel far. Either way, anyone breaches our perimeter and I'll know when those sirens on the fishing line go off, and they'll be the worse for it."

April seemed to relax a bit. For the first time, she had a clear view of the man who had rescued her. He was tall, at least six foot two. She imagined that at one time he was bigger and quite handsome, but now he was thin, perhaps only one hundred and eighty pounds. His skin was pulled tight against his cheek-bones and his eyes were cold. He wore a long beard and his hair was equally long. Though he dressed like some kind of soldier, he looked more like a rebel biker. Tattoos covered his arms, right down to his fingers and up to his neck.

"Where did you come from?" Cotton asked. "Northern Territory? One of the cities?"

"Northern Territory?" April asked, her confusion obvious.

"Just what I said," Cotton continued. "You know, the old Dakotas, Montana."

"Old Dakotas?"

"Why do you keep repeating everything I say?" Cotton asked. He looked at her for a moment and then canted his head to the side. "Where have you been for the past year?"

April looked around again, and Cotton could see that she was getting anxious.

"Hey," Cotton said and held up his hands in a placating gesture. "I ain't here to hurt you, but you need to understand something. If you're going to be around my daughter, I need to know who you are."

April took a deep breath and then nodded her agreement.

"I've been in a bunker."

CHAPTER 2

"MY FATHER WAS A SURVIVALIST, but he was doing it way before the virus came. He was an old school prepper from back in the Red Scare days. I remember when I was a little girl helping him bury supply caches in the woods around the house," April said as the trio sat in the glow of the red lantern. "That was why Mama left. Eventually. In the beginning, she was a part of it and was just as invested as he was because they all thought some Russian was going to press the button. Or maybe we would. Then the wall fell and the Soviet empire went away. I came along. That's when Mama decided she didn't want to live in Daddy's doomsday world anymore."

"I remember that," Cotton said with a hint of a

smile. "Getting under my desk in grade school in case a nuke went off."

"Maybe that would have been better than what really happened," April went on. "Mama left, but she didn't take me with her. So I stayed with Daddy. The more time I spent alone with him, though, the more I realized he needed someone to take care of him. That's what I did. Even helped him contract to dig out the bunker in the backyard."

"You had a real bunker?" Jean asked with wonder in her eyes.

"Yeah. Looking back on it, it wasn't the worst idea in the world," April said with a shrug. "I went on with life as best I could. Even went to nursing school. Maybe that was so I could be better at taking care of him. Thing about preppers, at least in my experience, is they seem to be good at taking care of everything in the world except themselves. Daddy was no different. His heart was failing long before the entire world did."

"You stayed with him," Cotton surmised.

"He didn't leave me much choice. When the riots started and people were getting sick, it was everything I could do to keep him out of that damn bunker. We were in the middle of nowhere so there wasn't any reason to go living in a hole." April paused for a moment, and her demeanor changed. "Then the vaccine came, and not long after that, they started going door to door with it. Then there was no stopping him from going into the bunker."

"You were there the whole time, weren't you?" Jean asked. She understood what had happened.

"Yes," April replied. "He had set it up for five years. It had air purification, water, food, hard drives full of movies, board games, everything you would need to survive."

"Wait..." Cotton said, his eyes searching. "You would have comms. You would have heard something."

"Comms went down in the first month," April said. "It wasn't just one thing, either. The system couldn't be fixed. There were interference problems with the concrete in the bunker, then the external antennae had a catastrophic malfunction. I even tried to go outside at one point and use my cellphone, but that didn't work either."

"Cyberattacks. When the people started pushing back against the government, a network of insurgent hackers started a 'Fire Sale,' meaning everything must go," Cotton explained. "Crashed the entire network for about two weeks. Even after that, it was spotty for a long time, going in and out. Now you can't get a signal outside of the cities unless you have a sat phone."

"That would explain it," April said. "I thought he was right. The only safe place was the bunker. I figured if the virus was spreading faster and people were getting sicker and sicker, we would... well..."

Cotton could see that she didn't want to say it. She didn't want to be the first one to say out loud what so many people had been thinking. What he had planned for.

"Wait them out," Cotton finished for her. "Wait for them to die."

April nodded.

"Daddy always said it would only take seventy-two hours after a societal collapse for people to turn on each other, and within a few weeks, seventy percent of the population would be dead."

"He wasn't far off," Cotton affirmed.

"I imagine he wasn't," April said. "So, we stayed put. We did the best we could to keep from going crazy. Went above ground and got some sunlight each day because they said Vitamin D was important if you wanted to survive the virus. I even did a little walk through the woods to get eyes on the next town over, you know... from a distance. Wanted to see if there was any activity, if maybe it might be safe to venture into town and at least try to get a new radio or some news."

"What happened?"

"Only made it about a mile before I heard engines and shouting. Didn't sound much like a group of folks I'd want to get to know better, so I headed back. That was six months ago."

Cotton thought about that timing.

"Yeah, that would have been after the government pulled out and officially started calling Texas a 'failed state' along with most of the states in the Meat Belt."

"Meat Belt?" April asked.

Cotton and Jean shared a look. This woman had no idea what had happened.

"We'll get to that in a minute," Cotton said. "When did you finally decide to leave the bunker?"

"Day after he died," April said. It was clear that she still had not quite processed her father's death. "He went quietly. In his sleep. We had just finished watching 'The Day After' for the hundredth time. You remember that? The mini-series from the eighties about a nuclear holocaust?"

Cotton laughed.

"Yeah, the one with Craig T. Nelson. My dad

used to watch that too. That and Shaka Zulu. Over and over again," he said.

"We never got around to Shaka Zulu, but that movie... something about it really got to him. That night, he told me he loved me. Told me I was a survivor and that if anything ever happened to him, I'd make it fine on my own."

"Do you think he knew? That he was dying?" Jean asked.

"Hard to say," April replied. "He wasn't a very spiritual person, wasn't very in tune with his body. I kind of doubt he would have had that level of intuition."

"What happened when you left?" Cotton asked, wanting to change the subject.

"I didn't even make it five hundred feet. I don't know if maybe they knew we were there and were just waiting on us to eventually stick our heads out or if it was just bad luck. That morning, I loaded up everything I thought I'd need to at least make it to town. Ruck sack with food and medical, Daddy's rifle and a handgun. I was almost to the tree line when they came at me from across the field on the other side. Don't know why in the hell I didn't leave at night."

"You had a rifle. Get any shots off?" Cotton asked.

"I... I hit the magazine release instead of the trigger," April said, clearly embarrassed.

Cotton laughed.

"Hey!" April snapped and then remembered to lower her voice. "Sorry I'm not a Green Beret or something! I was scared!"

"No," Cotton said. "I'm not laughing at you. I did the same thing the first time I drew down on a man."

"Really?" April asked. Her eyes were wide with disbelief.

"It's true. Back when things kicked off in Afghanistan, we weren't working as many of the fine motor mechanics. Mainly a lot of trigger pulling, but not enough time on weapons manipulation. We had guys dropping mags, going white light by accident, all kinds of shit. You ain't the first."

April smiled at that. She shifted in place a bit and shrugged.

"So, they took me."

She said nothing more. Cotton let the silence hang in the air and didn't push it. April parted her lips.

"You don't have to," Cotton said. "If you don't

want to. Everyone has a story now. Not all of them need to be told."

"It's okay," April said. "I don't mind. Honestly, there's not much to tell. Not really. They hopped out of their trucks and chased me across the field. That's all I remember. Must've overtaken me and knocked me out."

"Then you woke up somewhere else," Jean said.

"Yes," April said. "In a room. Like maybe it was an old warehouse or something. Lots of folks were in there, but no one said anything. Not a word. We barely even looked at each other. I caught on to that pretty quick. When folks are that quiet, there's a reason for it, so I didn't say anything either. Only time anyone would make a noise was when they started screaming. When the men came for them."

"What men?" Cotton asked.

"We always knew who they were, and why they were there. They were coming to take someone, or maybe a few people. They showed up wearing these... these leather aprons. They'd walk toward a person and the others would scatter. Kind of like, you know how cockroaches scatter when you turn on the light? It was like that. It was just like that."

"Where did they take them?" Jean asked.

"Can't really say I know," April replied. "All I know is that they never came back."

Jesus Christ, Cotton thought to himself. *She really doesn't know.*

"How long do you think you were there?" Cotton asked.

April shook her head.

"Don't know. Weeks maybe? Only a little bit of light got in through the cracks in the roof, but it was hard to keep track even with that. I know I lost weight. The stuff they would feed us, it just came in buckets. Tasted god-awful, but we learned to get it down. There was never enough though, never enough for a full stomach."

"Kept you weak," Cotton concluded. "Too weak to run."

"Except she did," Jean cut in.

"That night... that night was chaos. They'd brought some new people in and a few of them were young men. Normally they'd separate the younger ones but not this time. Maybe they just got lazy. When they walked into the warehouse, I could see it in their eyes right away, in the new ones. They knew it was bad. Knew it wasn't going to be anything they would come back from. They fought back, got a gun away from one guard and shot him, then another and then another. The doors were wide open, so people started running. I could see past them into a yard. Big open yard like maybe a cattle pen. Honestly, I don't even remember. Even when I was running through it, I couldn't process it.

"Then I felt something slam into my back. Still not sure what they hit me with. I went out for a minute, long enough for someone to get on top of me and tie my hands. Then I... I..." April reached up and touched her forehead. "I watched someone put an axe through his head. Right on top of me."

"But you didn't hesitate," Cotton said.

"I was so scared," April said. "My body just, it just sprang up like I was possessed. And then I could feel my feet running beneath me, almost like one of those out-of-body experiences you hear people talking about. Then I was just running."

"How far do you think you ran before they tracked you down?" Cotton asked.

"I ran all state in high school," April said. "Long distance. Tried it in college too but I wasn't good enough. I ran at least ten miles before I heard their trucks behind me again. Ran that whole time with my hands tied."

"You did the right thing," Cotton said. "You didn't have long left."

There was recognition in April's eyes. She realized Cotton knew something.

"Long left until what?" April asked. "What in the hell has been going on out here?"

Everyone knows how it started. It was just a flu, and not even much of a flu at that. At first, they said it only had something like a three percent mortality rate. If it wasn't anyone you knew, maybe that didn't seem so bad. Then it went to ten percent. Then the hospitals were going dark. Doctors were walking off the job because no one signed up for burning bodies in a parking lot, but that was what we saw. That was what they paraded all over the news.

I knew it was the end when I started seeing it in memes. A photo of stacks of bodies being burned with a clever tag line. We were losing our humanity too fast.

Society was coming apart at the seams. There were riots in most major American cities and the rest of the world wasn't faring much better. We were even hearing stories about twenty percent mortality rates in countries like Brazil and Argentina.

Then India caught fire. I mean, it really caught fire. All the talking heads had theories about why it went down the way it did over there. Maybe something to do with sanitation or the virus bonding to some bacteria and mutating. I'm not even sure how that all works, but I do know how it ended.

Fifty percent mortality rate in India. We were still holding at ten percent, but people panicked. One thing I know from all the years doing the work we did in the Teams, when people panic, they make bad decisions. Like ramming a vaccine through production in five months that should have taken five years. Minimum.

I know a lot of the experts, the real ones, not the ones the government bought, tried to warn everyone. They were shouting it from the rooftops, or at least the twenty-first century equivalent: Social Media. That should have been another warning sign when these people all started getting censored on the usual platforms. Then they were just outright banned. One day you're one of the most brilliant minds in the world, the next you're showing up in search results as a fringe lunatic.

They silenced anyone who disagreed with the way the government was handling the vaccine. There were even stories about people being permanently silenced. Like that Fluid Dynamics executive who threw himself off the roof of the corporate head-quarters building in New York City.

No one wanted to hear it. Honestly, the worst part about how it all went down was that it wasn't even about survival, not really. They just wanted their lives back. People probably weren't nearly as freaked out about those mortality rates as they were by the idea that things might never go back to the way they were.

So, they lined up for the vaccine. Lines that stretched out for freaking miles. It was the miracle vaccine, and they had a slogan which you saw everywhere. That should have been another red flag. Those three words were on billboards all over the country: Accept The Miracle. That was it. Nothing else. Just giant red letters on a black background.

I was working as a contractor at Dam Neck, teaching CQB at Development Group. That's what we called Seal Team Six. No one who's actually there calls it Seal Team Six. That's a good way to get laughed out of the room or get your ass beat.

One day the Command Master Chief called me in and handed me a chit for medical. It's filled out for me with all my info on it. It's a request for the vaccine. I asked him if this was a joke and he told me no, it's not and that the entire command was going into lockdown until everyone got their dose. He told me to take the chit and go to medical.

Keep in mind I'm a civilian contractor. I'd known this man for twenty years, and I'll never forget the look in his eyes when he handed it to me. It was fear. Then he mouthed a single word to me.

"Run."

I did. I walked out of the building, but instead of heading to medical; I went to my truck and left the compound. I didn't even go home. I picked up my little girl from her grandma's house and we headed to my cabin in West Virginia, where all of my gear and supplies were.

Thing about it is, I think that was the first time I saw it. My mom got her dose right away because she was in the risk group. She'd already had the vaccine for a month. I told her I loved her, but I knew she wouldn't come with me. I kissed her on the cheek and I looked her in the eyes. That's when I think I saw it, that white film on her eyes. Not full blown, not like it would get, but just the beginning of it.

That was the first reported side effect. There were others, all the usual stuff, but that was what made the news. About half of the people who took the vaccine, their eyes turned white but nothing else, so people didn't really start panicking yet.

By then, I fully set Jean and I up in my cabin. No one was going to find us, that was for damn sure. I didn't know what the plan was, not if I'm being honest about it, but I knew one thing: if anyone came around looking to stick that poison in my little girl's arm, they were going to have a very bad day.

Then the attacks started. When the first ones made the news, everyone thought it had actually come to zombies. Like, this was it. We've finally gone through the looking glass and are dealing with actual zombies.

That's not what it was, though. Maybe this was worse. Whatever you wanted to call it, the attacks were piling up. People were also being admitted to the hospital with stomach pain. Like crazy stomach pain. They were coming through the door doubled over and screaming. They were spitting up blood.

I say zombies would have been easier because I don't think it would mean much to kill them. They would just be, I don't know... husks or something. But these were normal people. Their eyes were glossed over with that white shit, but in every other way, they were normal.

Well, they were normal except—they wanted to eat other people. It didn't take long to figure out what was happening because of the attacks. They were... well; I guess they were cannibals. Like I said, it didn't take long to make the connection and figure out what was happening to these people flooding the hospitals in so much pain. They were starving.

It wasn't like normal starvation. It was fast. If they didn't get... you know, human flesh, they would expire within a matter of days. I don't quite understand all the science behind it, but there was something about an amino acid imbalance that caused them to consume their own tissues. The first stage of becoming a cannibal was actually consuming yourself, but you could stop it if you consumed someone else first.

The government acted fast. A little too fast, if you ask me. Bodies were stacking up again, but this time it was this self-cannibalization. They withered away to skin and bones within days if they didn't get that specific nutrition. The government had a fix ready. The FEMA distribution centers opened within two weeks of the first attacks. Two weeks. Think about that.

The fix wasn't really anything new. We had been growing meat in labs since 2013, but that was beef. Weird thing was, they did experiments growing meat from human cells just a couple of years ago. You would just take a swab from inside your cheek, grab a few cells and then grow the meat from there.

That's exactly what we did. No one knew when the hunger would kick in. It wasn't right away. For some people, it never did, just like not everyone got those milky white eyes. But that wasn't a risk anyone wanted to take.

At that point, between the original virus and what the vaccine was causing, we were at 25% mortality. There was a lot of other stuff going on too, but getting into all of that, we'd be here all night and never get to the bottom of it.

Let's just say things were deteriorating. The government enacted emergency powers, one of which was lifetime appointments for all serving politicians. The Republicans pushed back against this, but not that hard. It looked like a lot of theater. They bundled this into the Loyalty Pledge. If you wanted the boosters for the original vaccine and if you wanted sustenance, you had to sign the Loyalty Pledge.

Everyone signed it. Everyone. Maybe five percent held out.

I hoped that was going to be the end of it. We were still holed up in the cabin, just getting used to life in the woods. I was in contact with a few buddies from the old days who were doing the same thing, working that HAM radio, and I did my best to stay up on what was going on.

After the Loyalty Pledge, everything kind of went quiet. The riots seemed to calm down, the Consumers (that's what we called the people who'd gone cannibal and lived in the cities) were getting fed and the original virus seemed to be dying off.

Then everything exploded. It was fast. It was so fast. The original conversion rate from the vaccine had only seemed to be about twenty percent. That was the number of people that started craving human flesh. No one knows why it happened, but overnight, it jumped to one hundred percent. At that point, seventy percent of the country was vaccinated.

I grew up in church, just like any good southern boy. I remember sitting in the pew and reading the Bible. I did read the whole thing, but there was one part I read over and over again, the same one most little boys probably do: Revelations.

All the traffic I was getting on the net sounded like that. I didn't think there could be much time left. I thought we were close to everyone being killed off, either by the virus or by each other.

The government tried to get control again. For the first time since the Civil War, they deployed

Federal troops on American soil. We were in a full-blown Revolutionary War between what was left of the government and the Free People of the American Republic. That didn't last long. No one knew where the front line was, because there wasn't one. They also had a hell of a time getting the average eighteen year old soldier to fire on his neighbors or brothers.

Within a few weeks, the Federal government was basically destroyed, but they had taken a lot of the FPAR fighters with them. State governments tried to stabilize, but they also fell apart pretty quickly. It was the cities that figured it out. Specifically, the smaller ones that had little ground to defend. San Francisco, New York, Houston, New Orleans, places like that did pretty well. They just sealed up, circled the wagons, and established themselves as private entities.

They left everything else to rot. I'd guess about five percent of the country still has some version of a civilized society in the cities. They keep supplying the population with farmed human flesh and they maintain control.

The rest all became something out of Mad Max, for the most part. Different feudal kingdoms popped up, but very few were well organized, except out here in Texas where you have the King. Story goes that he's the one who took the shot that killed the President of the United States. Took that shot from two miles away, they said, because he knew that would be the tipping point. That everything would come crashing down. Maybe that was what he wanted. He also has his Kingsmen, the ones who enforce the treaty.

Treaty Members are another step down from there. Usually just random gangs, but they know the rules laid down by the King and they abide by them. They all know that any man who can shoot another man through the torso from two miles away, well, he isn't one you want to cross.

"You okay?" Cotton asked.

Since he had finished his recounting of what occurred while she was underground, April had sat stone-faced.

"I... I don't understand," April stuttered.

Cotton and Jean looked at each other and then back to their guest.

"Which part?" Cotton asked.

"Any of it!" April snapped, but then caught herself. "I'm sorry, I didn't mean that. I just don't understand how it all really happened. All the things

Daddy was always talking about, they always sounded so crazy, but this..."

Her voice trailed off into the darkness.

"This is way worse," Cotton finished for her.

"Yeah," April said. "I mean... where do we go from here?"

Cotton looked at his daughter again. She nodded.

"North," Cotton said. "That's the plan, at least as much as we've got. Heading for Alaska where we can get lost and the territory is too harsh for folks to come looking for us."

"How are you getting there?"

Cotton tapped his right boot with one of his abnormally long, tattooed fingers.

"You're walking?" April asked in disbelief. "How long does something like that take?"

"I figure about three months," Cotton said. "Depending on which route we take and how much truth there is to the stories I've heard on the net."

"Stories?" April asked.

Cotton seemed to think about this for a moment and then went on.

"There's a lot more going on in the world than just the virus and some... cannibals." It had taken him a moment to get the word out. Even by that point, Cotton Wiley himself was still having trouble accepting the reality of what had happened. "Certain countries took advantage of the chaos. The Chinese moved into India and Pakistan under the guise of offering humanitarian assistance. Then they never left. Pretty soon, they also moved into Afghanistan and other neighboring countries. Word has it that the Chinese North Sea Fleet isn't in the North Sea anymore. They're anchored off the coast of California. Just sitting there. Waiting."

"Waiting for what?" April asked.

Cotton shrugged.

"Opportunity? Hell, it would be a reasonable assumption that at this point you just have to wait us out. In the last eighteen months, any reliable estimate says the population of the United States is down by sixty percent."

"Jesus!" April gasped.

"Might be more," Cotton said. "There's just no way to know. Word also has it that the Chinese were moving up through Brazil sometime last year. Even the President of Brazil was on the radio telling everyone to buy rifles, all the citizens. Not the military. He thought they were going to be fighting to the last man, woman and child."

"Was he right?" April asked.

"Comms suck now," Cotton replied. "I get bits and pieces, but it's a big game of telephone. Plus, there are a lot of bad actors on the net, probably foreign influence spreading mis-information. Hard to know what's true or not. Like the Russians in Canada."

"Do you have alcohol?" April blurted.

Cotton laughed as he dipped into his rucksack and returned with a bottle of Old Grandad. He tossed it to her.

"Your stomach is probably messed up from what they fed you," Cotton said. "Take it slow."

April nodded as she uncapped the bottle and took a swig. She grimaced at the burn but took another, albeit smaller one, right away.

"Yeah, the Russians are in Canada," Cotton went on. "That one I'm sure about. They were building military bases in the arctic, way before the virus. Like something straight out of a James Bond movie. Everyone knew why they were doing it; we just didn't want to take any action. When things fell apart, they started using those as staging areas and came down from the north. Those Russkies, they don't mind the cold, don't mind the snow. They ate it for breakfast."

"Did the Canadians put up a fight?" April asked.

"Not really," Cotton said. "I'm sure they tried, but they just weren't set up for it. They never stood a chance. Way I heard it, they surrendered by the end of the first week. Seems like it went fairly peacefully. While the Russians were assaulting through Canada, South London was literally burning and the Americans were eating each other. The Canadians knew no one was coming to help them."

"But if the Russians are in Canada, won't you have to go through them to make it to Alaska?"

"No choice," Cotton said. "Can't stay here, that's for sure. At least if we can make it to Alaska, we have a chance." He looked at his daughter. "A chance at a future. If we stay here and get caught in the middle of a Russia/ China invasion, well... we all know how that story ends."

It was clear that there was something on April's mind, but she didn't want to come right out and ask it.

"I don't know if you can come with us," Cotton said. "At least not yet. You understand why, right?"

April nodded.

CHAPTER 3

COTTON WILEY WALKED out of the darkness carrying his rifle, NODs down and posture relaxed. He had performed one final security check before deciding it would be okay for them to get a few hours of sleep in this location prior to getting back on the road again.

Normally they slept during the day, often in an abandoned structure, though small vans were usually best as long as it wasn't too hot. If someone was out scouting for food or supplies, they rarely messed with vehicles for whatever reason. Maybe too much of a chance someone was inside that you wouldn't want to get in a fight with over a can of soup.

That wasn't the case with tractor trailers. Cotton had made that mistake early on and been awoken by

Jean's screams to find himself in a knife fight with three men who had thought they'd snuck up on them. That time, he woke up burying his fixed blade Winkler knife in the chest of a very surprised would-be looter.

That was how muscle memory worked, how training worked. It took over when you needed it. You woke up in a knife fight. Maybe you saw someone out of the corner of your eye and the next thing you know, a gun is in your hand and you find yourself standing over a dead body. Maybe in a lot of ways the training took over so that your more human side couldn't.

Sometimes Cotton wondered how much of that human side remained, and how much more he could afford to chip away before he was just another animal like all the others roaming the Texas Meat Belt.

Maybe that was one benefit of sleeping at night when they had that luxury. Perhaps something about closing his eyes in the darkness and feeling some semblance of safety made him feel a little more human.

Jean reached out and turned the small knob on the red lantern that increased the brightness. Not much, but just enough that they could make out the lines on each other's faces. Even hers. Even at twelve years old, this life had already carved its tale upon young Jean Wiley.

Cotton sat down on a stump and rested his rifle beside it. He had already powered down his NODs and flipped them up. Now he rubbed his eyes a little. He didn't want to admit it to himself, but it was getting harder and harder to look through them all night. A lot of guys developed eye strain and tension headaches from using night vision for extended periods of time. For whatever reason, he'd never had that problem, but now he could feel it creeping in. He wondered if it would get worse and if it did, how long he could keep going. Being able to travel and fight at night was a unique advantage in the hell ravaged landscape that used to be America. He couldn't lose that.

"Quiet out there?" April asked.

Cotton nodded. He looked to Jean. She was tired. He could see it in her eyes, but he knew she wouldn't say anything.

"You two should get some sleep," Cotton said. "We won't have long before we need to get moving."

"That's not how we do it," Jean countered. "You know that."

"Circumstance has changed."

"Negative," Jean said with a sly smile. "TTP, right?"

Tactics, techniques and procedures. These had been well established early on, and Cotton always slept first, so that if they were compromised and he had to fight, he wouldn't be running on empty.

"I've created a monster," Cotton said and returned the smile. "Fine. We'll stick with the TTP." He looked to April and then back to his daughter. "But if you think you're nodding off or—"

"Not my first rodeo," Jean shot back, and Cotton could tell that it wasn't all in good humor. Even though she was young, she already had too many nights like this under her belt. She didn't like her professionalism being questioned. "I know what to do."

Cotton nodded. He unrolled a tarp beside his rucksack and laid down. He didn't take his gear off, but instead only loosened the back strap on his Haley D3CRX chest rig. Just enough to let his lungs expand a little better, but not enough that it would slide off if he had to fight. Next, he disconnected the sling on his rifle from the front quick detach point, looped it around his right arm a few times and then connected it to a second QD point in the rear. In the unlikely event someone snuck up on him while he was asleep, there was no way they would snatch the rifle away without taking him with it. This trick went all the way back to his first military enlistment in the Marine Corps (before he moved to the Navy to try out for SEALs) and the First Sergeant at 1/8 who had a penchant for creeping around at night stealing rifles from Marines who were foolish enough to not secure them.

Once he had taken care of all his gear, Cotton performed one final task before closing his eyes. He pulled a roll of rigger's tape from his pack, tore off an eight-inch piece and then secured it over his mouth. With no more time wasted, he laid his head on the rucksack and went to sleep.

April had watched this whole ritual in silence, and once she was reasonably sure her rescuer had gone to sleep, she turned to Jean.

"Why did he tape his mouth shut?" April asked quietly, unsure if she should even ask the question.

"Sometimes he screams in his sleep," Jean replied. "He tapes his mouth shut so that if he does, it won't give us away."

April waited a beat before pursuing the question further.

"Why?"

"Why what?" Jean asked.

"Why does he scream in his sleep?"

"Not sure," Jean said with a shrug. "It started after he left the Teams. Day after, in fact. Almost like it was waiting or something, the screaming I mean. Daddy thinks maybe it has something to do with the explosives they used. Like... maybe his brain got a little spun around or something."

"Is he having nightmares?" April asked. "When he screams?"

"Can't say," Jean replied. "He never remembers what happens while he sleeps."

April studied the girl for a moment. There was a resolve about her, as if she knew what was coming. She knew what the future held for her and had accepted it. In that certainty, her only choice was to carry on. April wondered if she could do the same, if she had a similar quality within her. She didn't believe she did. Not after what had happened. She felt as if a fissure had developed in her spirit and it wouldn't take much to shatter it completely.

"How do you do it?" April asked.

"Do what?" Jean replied, her confusion obvious.

"Keep going," April said, and then looked out into the darkness. "Through all of this?"

"Got no other choice," Jean replied. She seemed to think about it for a moment and then went on. "Nothing lasts forever, not the good stuff or the bad stuff, either. Way I figure it, things have to turn around again at some point. We just have to keep going until they do."

"What if they don't?" April asked.

"They will," Jean replied insistently.

April looked into the young girl's eyes for a moment and then nodded. She surveyed the darkness beyond them and then turned back to Jean.

"Do you have... um..." April seemed to have trouble getting the words out.

"Ass wipe?" Jean asked and then laughed.

April nodded.

Jean dipped into her small pack and returned with a Ziploc bag stuffed with what looked like small tablets. She retrieved one from the bag and handed it to April, along with a small bottle of water.

"Where am I supposed to put this?" April asked cautiously.

"You don't put it anywhere, it's toilet paper."

April looked at the tablet.

"It is?"

"Compressed toilet paper," Jean clarified. "Just drip some water on it and it'll come apart."

"Smart," April said as she stood up.

"Take this too," Jean continued, and held out the little Springfield Hellcat pistol.

April stared at it for a moment.

"We're probably alone out here," Jean said. "But we may also not be. Better not to find out it's the latter and be up the creek without a paddle."

"Right," April said, and closed her hand around the pistol.

It was so quiet. April had only walked perhaps a hundred feet from the campsite, but she felt as if she were a world away. She looked around and saw nothing, only the darkness. She didn't imagine she was very far from where her father's bunker had been, but it was so much different. Everything was different.

Before, there had always been some ambient light in the sky from neighboring towns. Not as much as you might get if you were closer to a city like Austin, but enough that you noticed it. Enough that it broke the spell of the night. Now that was gone; and only darkness remained.

April had not asked for details about the power grid. That was something her father had talked about often, the "Grid Down" scenario that preppers considered their stock in trade. She had not asked for those details from Cotton because she didn't know how much more she could take, how much more doom her fractured spirit could handle.

Any question she may have had only required her to think of the worst plausible scenario, and that was most likely where they were at.

People were eating each other. Not only that, but society seemed to have accepted it. Wandering the wasteland, this "Texas Meat Belt" as Cotton called it, clinging to the possibility of freedom and some sort of future in Alaska, was as good as it was likely to get.

Who even was this man? A former SEAL and his daughter journeying north. Did Cotton even really know where he was going? More importantly, did he have a chance in hell of actually getting there?

There were so many uncertainties in this new world, but there was one reliable constant: the darkness. The nothing. Once you stepped into it and let it claim you, everything was done. It was the definition of finality.

She thought for a moment about why she had been out there, about what she should be doing, and then pushed it away from her mind. There was only one way out.

April reached down and pulled back the slide on the little Hellcat. There was a round in the chamber. Of course there was. These two were ready. They were ready for anything. At least, they seemed like they were. Even the girl. How was April supposed to make it out here, out in the Texas Meat Belt if she didn't even have the level of resolve possessed by a twelve-year-old girl?

She did not have that resolve. She wouldn't make it. Better to just finish it out there in the nothing and let it claim her. To step off the precipice and into the inky black.

April put the muzzle to her temple and closed her eyes, but it made no difference. The view was the same. She could feel her facial muscles tighten almost of their own accord in anticipation of what would come next.

She was going to do it. She was really going to. She had to. This was the only way to keep herself from hurting them.

"You'll go to hell," a voice called out of the darkness behind her. "Don't you know that?"

April gasped. The breath of air she had been holding in rich anticipation of what the afterlife would bring rushed out her lungs. She'd had two pounds of pull on the trigger when she heard Jean's voice. In her shock, April dropped the pistol to the ground.

She turned and could just barely make out Jean Wiley's face a dozen feet from her.

"What?" April asked.

"You'll go to hell," Jean repeated firmly. "It's in the scripture. If you take your own life, you'll be damned."

April wasn't sure what to say. She looked down to where the pistol had fallen in the dirt and then back to Jean.

"Aren't we already?" April asked. "Damned?"

Jean walked forward. She stopped, knelt down, and picked up the pistol. She checked the chamber just like her daddy had always taught her to do when receiving a firearm, and then she let the gun hang by her side.

"I'll do it for you," Jean said. "If you need me to."

"Do what?"

"Take your life," Jean said more quietly. "Daddy will hear the shot and he'll come, but he'll understand."

All in one moment, April was shocked, terrified, and ashamed. She was ashamed of herself. Ashamed that this young girl had so much more courage than she did. That Jean Wiley would do such a thing for a total stranger.

"I can't let you do that," April said.

"Why?" Jean pushed. "Because you don't want to put that on me or because you don't want to die?"

"Does it matter?"

"It always matters," Jean insisted. "World ain't getting easier, not anytime soon. Least not as I can see. If you're ready to die now just because some folks tried to turn you into dinner, best to get on with it. Don't waste your time and definitely don't waste ours." Jean unzipped the little fanny pack she was wearing and stuffed the pistol into it. "If you want to live, you're gonna have to fight for it. Starting right now."

Brian watched the first light of dawn break the horizon as he ran the final stretch toward the small town of Cypress Mill that he had come to only a few weeks prior. His heart pounded like it was going to beat out of his chest and his legs felt as if they were pumping battery acid instead of blood. He'd never run so hard or so far in his life, but he'd also never been so scared.

It should have been a simple job. Brian knew they would eventually call upon him to earn his keep and so he had volunteered for the hunting party because nothing ever happened on them. It was a glorified hike out into the central Texas Meat Belt. He'd shoot the shit with the boys, maybe pick up some supplies and ultimately come home with dinner.

That was the way it went. That was how this one should have gone. Until it didn't.

If he hadn't been rooting around in the back of that minivan looking for a gun, he would be dead, too. The van had been sitting on the side of the road with one of those stickers on the back that said "Glock Inside" like the old Intel logo. Seemed like a pretty dumb ass way to get your gun stolen out of your car, so Brian figured he might as well be the one to do the stealing. After all, it wasn't like the owner was going to be hanging out in there and if he was, he probably wouldn't be too lively.

Brian was like most people before the world fell apart. He wasn't a bad guy, wasn't a criminal. Not like some guys in the community were. He even went to church, for all the good that ended up doing him. Even if God had been listening when he was in church on Sundays, the man upstairs sure as hell wasn't listening now, at least not from what Brian could tell.

It had taken a few minutes working with the pry bar to get the back door of the minivan open. That was enough time for the rest of the boys to get well ahead of him going after that girl. He told them he'd catch up.

Then he heard the shots. He knew what they were. A friend of his had a suppressor on his hunting rifle, so Brian knew what it sounded like. Then there were screams. Then some talking and another shot. Brian had just stood there in the darkness. He didn't move. Not an inch. Even his breathing slowed down. He didn't know why he thought this, but he had the sense that whoever was out there could see him, and that if he started moving around or running, it would be the last thing he did.

Then he heard the girl talking to someone. He didn't know who. Finally, the talking stopped and Brian still waited for a few more minutes before moving, staying close to the cars stranded on the Interstate.

All those cars were there, not because zombies attacked them or some crazy nonsense like that. It was for the most benign reason possible. They'd just run out of gas. A lot of folks tried getting out of the cities even after the gas stopped flowing, but they didn't get very far. There were thicker clumps where military barricades had stopped them. That was a different story. Brian didn't like seeing those. These were people the government had lumped in as being aligned with the FPAR Revolutionaries, with predictable consequences. This had become a convenient way for the Federal Government to clean up groups of people that they couldn't quite figure out what to do with.

Inconvenient people became insurgents. Insurgents were the enemy.

In the areas where the cars had run out of gas, there were no people, there were no bodies. They had gone off on foot to find some refuge. At the military barricades, vehicles were piled up bumper to bumper. Heavy machine guns had blown out most of the windshields and the cars were packed with the dead.

There was a uniqueness to the horror Brian had felt the first time he came upon one of these scenes, because he wasn't even sure what he was looking at. They didn't look... human. It looked like a mix of bone and fruit jello had blown apart inside of the vehicles. The heavy machine guns the military had used, the fifty cal and the MK 19, that was what they did to people. The MK19 was a machine gun that fired 40mm grenades. These weapon systems weren't intended to be used against humans, they were normally deployed to defeat vehicles and armor.

Instead, they were used to stop these "Dangerous Insurgents" who were seeking to upset the balance of power that was keeping everyone safe. At least, that was how the Federal Government put it, and enough people believed the lie that it went unopposed.

Finding those cars full of bone and jello had been a big part of what finally drove Brian to join the community of Treaty Members out at Cypress Mill.

Brian had walked in the dark until he came upon the first body in the road. It was Mark, one of the guys who was former military. Brian remembered because Mark wouldn't stop talking about it. Seemed like he thought he knew everything about fighting and patrolling. Turned out he maybe didn't know as much as he thought he did.

Brian felt bad the moment this thought came to his mind. Even if this guy had been a bit of a pain in the ass, he didn't deserve to go out like this.

It was as Brian knelt there looking at the body

and then moved to the next one that he understood these men had run into something more than just some survivalist with a suppressed hunting rifle. Every shot was right between the eyes, and the shooter was definitely running military grade ammunition. It hadn't key-holed and made a messy entry wound like some of their cheap ammo often did.

The entire hunting party was dead. That sudden realization sent a charge through Brian. He felt his adrenaline surge and instantly turned and started running. He moved so fast he almost forgot to grab a pistol and some ammo off one of the dead men. As a new guy, he hadn't rated a gun, which was why he'd been so intent on finding the Glock that was supposedly 'inside' that minivan. Now he had one.

The sound of his boots slamming against the pavement seemed to sync up with his pounding heartbeat as Brian ran through the dawn and saw the jack-knifed big rig that blocked the main road into Cypress Mill.

He could also see the small sniper hide on top of the big rig, and he knew that one of the men would already have his scope's reticle on the young man's chest. He hoped to hell it wasn't that trigger-happy son-of-a-bitch, Fred.

Brian stopped and began waving his hands. He was close enough for a positive identification from the spotter who would no doubt be laying prone beside the shooter.

"Wait," Jorge said and touched Fred's shoulder.

"For what?" Fred asked, clearly annoyed by the interruption. He already had a decent amount of pull on the trigger and was interested to see if he could shoot out this kid's left eye. At three hundred meters with a half decent Athlon scope, it wouldn't be much of a challenge.

"I'm pretty sure it's that idiot kid that went out on the hunting party with Xander."

"Bullshit," Fred shot back. "Don't look a thing like him."

"It's *him*," Jorge replied insistently. "And if he's here alone, that ain't good."

Brian followed Jorge into the kitchen of the small farmhouse and then stood at some semblance of "attention" like he'd seen soldiers do in movies. It turned out it had been that trigger-happy so-and-so Fred on the gun, and it was likely that Jorge had saved Brian's ass.

Jorge had been the first one Brian met when he walked up on Cypress Mill weeks prior. The man had been tough on him, but had also treated him fairly. Brian appreciated this, and it was more of a fair deal than most people got in this new world.

Now they were meeting with the big boss; Randall Eisler. That was how everyone said his name, too. No one ever called him Randall, or even Mister Eisler. He was Randall Eisler. It also seemed that Randall Eisler liked it that way.

"You know what I really hate about being a cannibal?" Randall Eisler asked without looking up. Brian wasn't sure if he should answer or not, so he kept his mouth shut. Randall Eisler looked up and met his eyes. "Because that's what we are, in case you hadn't said it out loud lately. We're cannibals, right?"

This time, it was clearly a question.

"Yes, sir," Brian answered.

"Well... Brian, right?"

"Yes, sir," Brian said.

"Randall Eisler, if you don't mind."

"Yes, Randall Eisler."

"Well, now it just sounds weird. But... anyway.

What I hate about being a cannibal is that I can't taste eggs." Randall Eisler looked down at the eggs neatly laid out alongside two strips of bacon on a plate in front of him. "Can't taste much of anything really, aside from human flesh and alcohol. Every Sunday morning though, I try. I have 'em cooked for me with some bacon. I sit down at this table and for who knows how many times it's been now, I don't taste a thing. Just tastes like... I don't know. Not much of anything." He paused for a moment and looked at the eggs almost as if he were in mourning. He looked up at Brian from behind his milky white eyes. "Do you know why I do it? Why I sit down here every Sunday morning hoping for a different outcome?"

"No," Brian said.

"Because I'm fucking crazy," Randall Eisler said with a grin."But that's not the only reason. It's also to remember that we're still human. That we're not savages like those sorry sons of bitches out there wandering the Meat Belt. To remember that even if we're cannibals, we still remember a world without, well... us."

Brian said nothing.

"And to know it's Sunday," Randall Eisler said with a smile. "Because it's like Groundhog Day around here, unless something bad happens. So, tell me young man. What's the bad thing that happened out there?"

Brian relayed his story, or at least what he knew of it, while Randall Eisler listened patiently. When the young man had finished, Randall Eisler considered what he had just been told before following up.

"How can you be sure it was just one man?" Randall Eisler asked.

"I just heard the one voice," Brian replied. "Talking to the girl."

"Seem like she went willingly?"

"Near as I can tell. She didn't scream or nothing."

Randall Eisler seemed disappointed by this.

"Xander wasn't some slouch," Randall Eisler said, indicating the man who had been leading the hunting party. "He was the real deal. Shouldn't have been easy to take down. One man sure as hell shouldn't have aced him. If it was... well, that's something we'll need to run up the flagpole."

Brian felt a shock of fear race up his spine. Randall Eisler was a lot like Jorge. Tough but fair. He'd let Brian know from the time he first walked into the farmhouse weeks earlier that he'd get a fair shake as long as he did the work and did his best to uphold The Treaty.

The King, though. That was different. Was Randall Eisler asking him to take this to the King? Brian erred on the side of caution and said nothing.

Randall Eisler turned to Jorge, who had been standing silently behind Brian.

"Can you take him?" Randall Eisler asked.

"Rather not," Jorge said with a sly smile. "If it's all the same to you."

"Well, it ain't all the same to me!" Randall Eisler snapped. He caught himself and relaxed his posture. "Sorry. You didn't deserve that."

"No skin off my back," Jorge replied coolly. "I'll do it if you ask."

"Oh, I ask," Randall Eisler said firmly. "We've got a good thing going here, you know that. I aim to keep it that way. I know that you also understand keeping his highness happy is a big part of that."

Jorge didn't respond at first, and he could feel Randall Eisler boring holes into him with his stare.

"I get it," Jorge said.

Jorge stood a good six foot four and was not a small man. It was clear he had seen his share of manual labor and was not someone who cared to be pushed around. Even so, he knew when to toe the line.

"Good," Randall Eisler replied. "It shouldn't be anything but the proverbial chicken wing. Just drive our young friend up to Oatmeal, let him tell his tale and then you should be on your way."

Randall Eisler sat back in his chair and further contemplated his eggs and bacon for a moment before Jorge's shooting partner Fred walked to him holding a sealed envelope. Fred had been standing quietly while Brian relayed his story. Now he dropped this envelope on the table in front of Randall Eisler. On the front was the seal of the City State of Houston.

Randall Eisler looked at it for a moment and then up to Fred.

"It came through?" Randall Eisler asked.

"Just 10 minutes ago at the South Gate. Entire case of it delivered courtesy of our benevolent bene-factors."

Randall Eisler ripped open the envelope. He dropped the papers it held onto the table and ran his thumb down the manifest.

"I'll be a son-of-a-bitch," he said. "There it is in

black and white. Generation Two Pandemify, brought to you by your friends at Fluid Dynamics."

"Making America well again," Fred said, reciting the marketing slogan the company had used early on to promote the vaccine known as Pandemify.

"I did like 'Accept The Miracle' better," Randall Eisler mocked. "Either way, we've got thirty doses of it now to disperse as we please."

"How about into the toilet?" Fred asked, only half-joking.

"I'm not going to say I wouldn't like to, but it wasn't a load of shit, you know? What I said to the young man about us being more than just a bunch of cannibals."

"I know," Fred said.

"This is part of that. We have to give people the choice. If this stuff really can make them human again, that has to be their decision to make. Not ours."

"How do we handle the fallout?" Fred asked. "If they choose to take it."

"These are our friends and neighbors," Randall Eisler said. "In some cases, it might be folks we've fought side-by-side with. Way I figure it, a twenty-four-hour head start is the right thing to do."

"Food and gear?" Fred inquired.

"Food and gear," Randall Eisler said with a nod. "Get 'em set up right and then open the gate."

"Well, hopefully it's a moot point and no one will take it," Fred replied.

"Nah," Randall Eisler said. "Something we should have learned by now is someone will always take it. Doesn't even matter much what it is. Someone will always opt-in."

Fred seemed as if there was something else on his mind.

"Thoughts?" Randall Eisler asked.

"Well, it's just that we're doing all this ground-work for Houston. You know, we send them intel reports each day by radio. We take down FPAR if we find them. I'm just not sure what we're getting out of this deal aside from some vaccine we don't want."

"I understand your concern," Randall Eisler said. "But they're a government and they're a growing one. They have a lot more potential to consolidate power and spread their tentacles than New York or San Francisco do. Particularly since San Francisco is likely to get steamrolled by the Chinese sooner rather than later."

"So, we're staying on Houston's good side?"

"For now," Randall Eisler said with a nod. "More

than that, we're finding out everything we can about them and how they do things."

"So that when the time comes, we can fight back," Fred said, understanding what he had missed.

"Exactly."

Jorge closed the door after he had exited the house with Brian and let out a breath.

"We really going?" Brian asked.

"Of course we're going!" Jorge snapped. "What choice do we have?"

Brian wasn't sure how to respond.

"You ever been?" Brian asked. "To see the King, I mean."

"Yeah," Jorge replied as he led the way to his truck. "I used to work for him."

CHAPTER 4

IN THE BEGINNING, Cotton and his daughter had moved more tactically as they travelled first from West Virginia and then through the south. They had also been driving his truck, and that had meant sticking mostly to back roads and only hitting major thoroughfares if they had no other option.

Then, around the time they hit Tennessee, it was becoming more and more apparent that traveling by vehicle was a bad idea. By then the gas had dried up. Refineries had shut down months earlier, but that wasn't even the real problem. You could still pull whatever fuel you needed from gas stations or even the cars stranded on the roads if you didn't mind the taste of gasoline and were handy with a siphon.

No, the real problem was that by then a vehicle

(particularly fully loaded) was a moving target for marauders. Even though walking took a lot longer, you could at least keep a low profile and were more likely to reach your destination. You were also a much less attractive target than Cotton's old Toyota FJ loaded with supplies.

That was when the hard decisions started. Cotton could carry a lot on his back, that was nothing new, but even between his ruck sack and Jean's much smaller pack, they had little room for personal comfort items. Many things had to be ditched on the side of the road. In a strange way, this was the moment that Cotton really understood how fast Jean was growing up. She didn't complain about losing most of her clothes or her books. She understood those things would not get them where they needed to go.

That was also when Cotton left behind his armor. No more Ops Core ballistic helmet and Crye SPC with Hesco plates. The young SEAL in him had wanted to push back against that idea. He'd carried that weight and a hell of a lot more over the razorback mountains of Afghanistan. Not only had he carried it, but had then shown up fresh on target and engaged in some of the most intense assaults of his career.

The reality of aging told a different story. This meant no more armor and no more long gun with a Night Force scope. Instead of tossing these things on the side of the road, he buried them and marked the location on his map. That damn scope alone had cost nearly four thousand dollars. That was one piece he wasn't willing to give up, so he separated it from the rifle and stuffed it in his pack.

Now he was running slick with just his bump helmet to mount his NODs and his chest rig to carry magazines and other tools. Were it not for the need to mount his night vision to something, he would have ditched the helmet as well.

After Tennessee, they were a lot lighter and, sometimes, even moved faster than they would have in a vehicle. They didn't need to stick to main roads and could often cut a straight line from one point to another by going through the woods or over a small mountain.

When they first started walking, they stuck to smaller roads and often walked along the tree line to avoid detection. By the second week, Cotton understood that there weren't many people left to find them.

In the beginning, there had been a lot more people out, even some government agents and military hunting for the FPAR rebels. Then one day there weren't.

This led them to the interstate. At first, the idea of walking out in the wide open made Cotton a little nervous, not really for himself but for his daughter. However, after a few days of not running into a single soul, he understood they were safe out there. Maybe even safer than they had been in the tree line.

If someone was going to mess with them, he'd see them coming a mile away and put them down before they got close. Food was also less of a problem. Many of the vehicles scattered across the roads were still stocked with supplies. This was particularly true when they came upon one of the military barricades.

For those, Cotton had stopped his daughter, taken a knee and looked her in the eyes.

"I have to do something," he said quietly. "You're not going to like it."

"What is it?" Jean asked, craning her neck to look past her father.

From where she stood, she could see stains on the ground. Maybe it was water or some kind of oil, but it looked reddish. Beyond the cars, she could see a tank parked in the middle of the road.

Cotton reached into his pocket, retrieved a strip of cloth, and held it out.

Jean frowned.

"I don't like it," she protested. "Whatever it is, I can handle it. I'm twelve-years-old!"

"I know," Cotton said with a smile. "It's not for you, fancy face. It's for me. I know you can handle seeing it, but I can't handle you seeing it."

Jean grudgingly nodded her approval and closed her eyes. Cotton tied the blindfold across her face and then stood back up. He reached out and took her hand.

The two walked through the tangled maze of cars. Cotton had seen these barricade points before, but only from a distance through binoculars. He had purposely steered their path around them. This was different. Walking through this hell was different.

The cars were mostly destroyed, as well as the inhabitants. Red covered everything. Broken bodies hung through car windows, barely identifiable as human beings. It wasn't the first time Cotton had seen something like this. He'd done this in Iraq. Not to civilians, not to women and children, but to a truck full of ISIS fighters on their way to an ambush.

He could feel the tackiness of old dried blood under his boots with each foot step. It wasn't like fresh blood that was slick.

Cotton stopped in his tracks and looked down at the pavement in front of him.

A stuffed unicorn toy lay on the hot concrete, glued to the pavement in a sticky red pool.

"What is it?" Jean asked as her father stood motionless.

"Nothing," Cotton replied. "Just something on the road."

That was what had led them to this place, walking through central Texas straight down the Thirty-Five. Into the heart of the Texas Meat Belt.

Cotton had first heard people talking about this place months earlier, and it wasn't just Texas. The Texas Meat Belt really stretched from Louisiana clear out to New Mexico. Someone had given it that nickname and it stuck. It stuck because aside from New Orleans and Houston, there was no civilization out there. It was also understood that any unvaccinated person who ventured into this territory was likely to end up on the dinner plate.

The Meat Belt had the highest number of cannibal attacks in the country by a factor of ten. Even the Federal Police (what remained of them) stayed out. This was what led to all the Cities declaring Texas to be a 'failed state.' This was really just a lot of political theater because America itself was a failed state and had even been declared so by the United Nations. At least, what was left of the United Nations.

Only America had cannibals. No other country had taken that generation of the vaccine from that specific bio-tech company. All other countries had banned travel to or from the United States, not that anyone would want to go there. Not anymore.

The one exception to this was the foreign fighters that had been showing up over the past several months. No one was one hundred percent sure why they were there or who had sent them, but they were clearly on their way someplace. Cotton had come across a group of them in Arkansas and had recognized them from their ethnicity and kit as possibly being Polish, but he kept his distance.

Whatever they were up to, it was none of his business.

Normally Cotton and Jean would have travelled at night under NODs, but getting in that skirmish with the Treaty Members the night before had meant Cotton needed some rest before traveling again. They wouldn't walk too far during the day, particularly in the unseasonable October heat. The sun was already doing quite a number on their energy levels, so they would look for somewhere to hole up before noon, before it was right overhead, beating down on them.

Traveling light (after ditching most of their gear in Tennessee) meant that they mainly had food, water, ammunition and medical. The water was the tricky part because water is reasonably heavy, weighing about eight pounds per gallon. Cotton had found that he and Jean could get by on a gallon a day if they were covering a lot of distance and working pretty hard, but that was on a day when the temperature was reasonable. As he wiped another towel full of sweat from his brow, he imagined the temperature was pretty far from reasonable. Probably damn close to one hundred degrees, if not hotter.

Because water was so heavy relative to food or ammo, they only carried two gallons, three at the most. They could usually replenish this on the road from natural water sources or because it seemed to rain all the damn time in central Texas. Except they hadn't done that the other night, for obvious reasons.

Now they were down to just over a gallon. Not only that, but they had a third member in their party. That gallon would not last long.

He stopped and turned to where Jean and April

were walking just behind him. Jean looked pale and her eyes were heavy.

"You drinking water?" Cotton asked.

Jean hesitated.

"Answer the question," Cotton pressed and raised an eyebrow.

"It's just I know we're short," she stammered.

Cotton reached to his belt and pulled loose the canteen that was clipped there. He tossed it to her.

"Drink," he ordered. "We only have one IV bag. Don't want to waste it because you went down from dehydration."

"Yes, Daddy," Jean replied and dutifully took a swig from the canteen.

"How about you?" Cotton asked, directing the question to April.

"I could use a drink," April said.

She took the canteen from Jean and had a pull.

Cotton watched her drink. Something was off. It was one of those things that maybe the brain sees, but you don't quite process. He'd run into this before in combat. Something his brain registered, but he didn't understand until much later. He realized that his hand was hovering over the butt of his Glock 17. What in the hell was it?

Cotton relaxed his fingers and dropped his hand.

It was the heat. That's what it was. It was causing his mind to play tricks on him. He looked up at the sun and then back to April and Jean. He looked around and saw a lone house in the distance, set about a mile back off the interstate.

It looked like the perfect place to lie low for a while.

"We need to get out of this heat."

It had been a good decision to head for the house. Cotton knew it the moment they hit the long gravel driveway that led up to the old two-story structure. He knew this because each of his legs felt like it weighed five hundred pounds and his pants were already soaked through with sweat and it was only ten in the morning.

He wished to hell he'd had the sense to carry some sort of temperature sensor with him because while it was common for central Texas to hit even one hundred and fifteen degrees at the height of summer, this felt even hotter than that and it was the fall. Maybe the sun was getting ready to explode. This wouldn't surprise him. One more problem to add to the list.

He held up an open hand, the sign for Jean to

stop but not freeze. The girl knew all of her hand and arm signals by now, and more than once, it had saved both of their lives.

Cotton let out a breath and looked around. There were several old oak trees on the property, and he signaled for her to move to the one on the far left of the house. That was where they would grab some concealment while he performed a hasty recon of the property and then checked the interior of the house.

Jean led April toward the tree, quietly explaining what they were doing as Cotton began making his way around the structure.

There was a field of tall grass on the back side of the property and several live oak trees scattered around. The west side of the property sloped down into a steep ravine. Cotton made a mental note of that. If someone was going to come at them, that was how they would do it. Patrol down into that ravine and then come up over the top. He knew this because that was how he would do it.

By the side of the house Cotton found what he was looking for. He knew there would be one on a property this far out. It was just a question of where it would be.

Cotton walked across the backyard and stopped at the old well. It must have been there for damn near a hundred years. It was an old stone build with the hand crank to pull a bucket up. No doubt the rest of the house drew its water supply from it. If this was the case, they might even get to take a shower. That would be a hell of a thing.

He opened the cover of the well and worked the hand crank until the bucket came up. It was filled with water. Cotton leaned forward and inspected it. There was nothing weird in it and it looked clear enough, but he needed more than that. He'd already almost poisoned himself in Arkansas drinking from a river. Fortunately, Jean had seen the dead deer wedged against some rocks upstream and he'd spit the tainted water out in time. The worst thing about that incident was that he couldn't even blame ignorance. He'd just been lazy and almost paid for it with his life.

Cotton lifted his rifle and pointed the barrel into the well. He hit the Surefire Scout light and illuminated it. Nothing. He could see the water below and nothing was floating in it. Next, he slung the rifle and dropped his pack. He rooted around for a moment until he found the Ziploc bag with the water test strips then pulled one out and dipped it in the water.

He stared at the strip for a moment until it changed and showed that the water was clean.

Without hesitation, Cotton picked up the bucket and dumped it over his head, then dropped it back down the well and refilled it.

He wanted to call Jean and April over to get a drink, but he knew that would be sloppy. He needed to clear the house first.

Right away, he knew that whatever had happened in the house; it wasn't anything good. The smell hit him like a hammer to the face. Some folks talked about getting used to the smell of the dead, but that wasn't the case for Cotton Wiley, and he had seen and smelled plenty of them, both before and after the virus.

Even during the day, the house was fairly dark. He briefly considered hitting his light, but decided that would be overkill. It was there if he needed it, but there was no reason to announce his presence with a beam of blinding light if he didn't have to.

Cotton moved from room to room and it was all reflex from how many thousands of structures cleared he had no idea. Finally, he hit the end of the second floor and stopped. Nothing. No one. It was empty. Yet the smell remained. No. He was missing something.

He brought his rifle up from the low ready and moved back down to the second floor. What was he missing? He snaked his way through the first floor again, but still nothing. No one. He went back out the front door and that was when he saw it. The doors to the storm cellar. They were on the exterior of the house and locked from the outside with a heavy chain and padlock.

The chains were rusted through and seemed to have been like that for a while. He wanted to just leave it alone. Whatever had been chained in there most likely wasn't going anywhere. Most likely, but that wasn't a certainty. Leaving it would be sloppy.

What he wouldn't give for some mechanical breaching tools. He had a single breach pen that he could use to cut through the chains silently, but this wasn't the time or place to spend such a valuable commodity. Instead, he stepped back, scanned his surroundings again, and put a 5.56 round through the lock. With the suppressor on his rifle, it was unlikely anyone would have heard that from very far away. It was a risk to reward problem. Here, the potential reward exceeded the risk.

Cotton stepped forward and cleared the chains from the door. He threw them open and hit his rifle light, which flooded the cellar. He took a step back.

The smell that had hit him in the face like a hammer in the house now had the stopping power of a locomotive. He moved forward again and went down the steps. He stopped.

"Jesus," he whispered.

This was where they had done it. Perhaps they had been ashamed, and that was why they locked it up before they left. They had left because there was no more food.

It was a butchery. There were remains of bodies scattered across the dirt floor of the cellar. Mostly bone, but some seemed more recent. That was strange to him because of the way the chains on the outside had rusted. There were blood spatters across the walls. Some bodies were small.

Cotton felt his legs give out from beneath him and he fell to a seated position on the steps.

For a moment, he just sat and stared at the carnage. How in the hell had they gotten to this point? He knew he couldn't let himself get pulled into that rabbit hole, wrapped up in that thought process. It always took him in the wrong direction.

Cotton let out a breath and stood back up. He did one more scan of the basement. There was nothing.

. . .

Jean stood in the shade of the live oak tree and swatted at the occasional bug that landed on her skin. The shade felt good and for a moment she forgot how thirsty she was. She had a bottle of water in her small pack but held off on taking another drink from it. She was sure her daddy would find water soon, probably even in that house, but she didn't want to chance it.

She watched April. The woman appeared to be perpetually on the verge of something. Jean just couldn't tell what that something was. April seemed uncomfortable in her own skin. She swatted at the same bugs that were tormenting the younger girl.

"Bugs grow big in Texas," Jean said with a smile. "Like everything else I guess."

"Where did you come from?" April asked. "If you don't mind me asking."

"West Virginia." Jean paused for a moment. "Well, Momma was from Virginia, the regular kind. That's where I stayed a lot with Grandma, but Daddy says it's really all the same."

"Did they have bugs this size in West Virginia?" April asked.

"Bigger," Jean assured her. "Carry off a grown woman if you don't watch out."

April laughed and then swatted at a particularly aggressive bug that flew into her eye.

"Damn it!" April shouted and turned to Jean. "That one got me good."

Jean felt her blood run cold. She wanted to freeze, but knew that she wouldn't. She did just as her father taught her and took three steps back as she pulled the Hellcat pistol from her fanny pack and aligned the sights on April.

"Do not move!" Jean shouted. "I will kill you! I promise you!"

For a moment, April was confused, even horrified. Then she understood what had happened.

Jean looked up at the woman, specifically into her left milky white eye. It wasn't the entire eye, but April's contact lens had slipped just enough to reveal her true nature.

"Wait!" April begged, holding up her hands. She felt a panic seize her. This girl would indeed shoot her. She could see it in young Jean Wiley's eyes. April also knew that she wouldn't be the first person this young woman had gunned down.

"Daddy! Daddy! Daddy!" Jean screamed.

. . .

Cotton tore through the backyard with his rifle short stocked over his shoulder. It would be fast. He knew it would. The second a target came into view, he would slide the rifle forward, rotating the stock back into a vertical position. He would slam it into his shoulder at the same moment that his eye picked up the EOTech reticle, his thumb flicked off the safety and his index finger took up the slack on the trigger.

When he saw his daughter holding a gun on April, the sequence did indeed unfold just as he knew it would, all but the last piece. His finger never broke the wall of the trigger. Something was wrong. Cotton slowed his stride but kept the reticle of his holographic weapon sight on April's face. She looked just as panicked as Jean did. Even more so.

Then he saw it. He saw what his little girl had. He saw the eye.

"On your knees!" Cotton shouted, so forcefully that it took even Jean off guard.

April stumbled back as if the words had been physically forceful enough to knock her off balance.

"Please!" April pleaded. "I—"

"Now!" Cotton shouted. "Get on the ground!"

April complied, but it was more of a stumbling action than a willful obedience, as if her legs had given out beneath her. She could feel her hands trembling uncontrollably as the adrenaline surged through her system. This was it. This was her time to die. She knew it. This man would be her executioner. Her weeks of living in constant fear after emerging from the bunker were about to be at an end.

"Move back baby," Cotton said more gently, waving his daughter back.

Jean lowered her pistol and walked backward to the tree.

"It's better if it's fast," Cotton said, now directing his words to April. "Just close your eyes. I'll make it fast."

"No!" April shrieked. "I don't want to die."

"I'm sorry," Cotton said quietly as he picked up the slack on his trigger.

"I can tell you where they are!" April shouted.

Cotton paused.

"Why do I care?" He asked.

"They're in your path," April said. "Probably. If you're heading north. A town called Oatmeal. That's where the King is. He's got too many people. You might miss them and you might not. I can tell you how to avoid them."

Cotton thought about it for a moment. Then he

brought his rifle up lightning fast, took up the slack again, and broke the trigger.

"Down!" He shouted.

Cotton stepped forward, dropped his knee into April's back and pushed her into the dirt.

Jean had already flattened herself to the ground as her father spun to the right and hit his next target.

Two men lay dead in the dirt, both armed with AR-15 rifles. They were well equipped with chest rigs, spare mags, and even comms. One more emerged from the tall grass, rifle shouldered and ready to take a shot, but he was no match for Senior Chief Cotton Wiley.

Cotton broke two more shots, one to the head and another to the chest of the third man.

He grabbed April from the ground and shoved her toward the house.

"Go! Now!" He shouted.

Jean followed by leaping from the dirt and breaking into a dead sprint. On her way, she grabbed April by the sleeve and pulled her along. The woman had been stumbling almost in a circle, clearly in a state of extreme panic and disorientation between almost being executed by Cotton and now facing this new threat. She followed Jean up the steps and heard zipping noises past her head, then saw the wood doorframe splinter. They were being shot at.

Cotton moved to the oak tree and took cover as more men emerged from the tall grass. Three more and they knew where he was. Rifle rounds hammered into the tree trunk as Cotton held his position. Then another round struck the tree beside his head and he turned to his left.

"Son-of-a-bitch!" He whispered as he slapped the flip to side magnifier in place and acquired his target. "It's a trap."

The 3x magnifier allowed him to see clearly much further away through the EOTech holographic weapon sight. A single shooter was coming up out of that damn ravine, just like he knew they would. Cotton lined up his reticle on the man's head and sent him the good news.

He watched the shooter fall to the ground and saw yet more figures coming up out of the ravine. The men coming out of the tall grass were advancing, so he took the only option left.

Cotton quickly switched out the magazines on his M4, loading a fresh mag with the requisite thirty rounds. He stepped out from behind the tree and laid down the fastest suppressive fire he ever had in his life. There is an art to shooting that fast from a semi-automatic AR-15 platform. Contrary to what the general public believes, AR style rifles do not just shoot an endless stream of bullets if you hold down the trigger. That privilege is reserved for the military, and even then they only fire three round bursts. If you want to shoot fast with a civilian AR, you learn to feel the reset of the trigger as you release it and immediately break the wall again. Someone who can do this, who can really master the art and science of fast shooting, is a terror to behold.

Cotton Wiley was just such a man, and this tactic had the desired effect. As the first magazine emptied, Cotton hit the release, swapped in a new one and hit his bolt release to send the bolt forward and chamber a new round. There was almost no break in his rate of fire. He was that fast.

The men who had emerged from the tall grass retreated. To put a finer point on it, they turned tail and ran in terror.

Cotton moderately slowed his rate of fire as he moved backward toward the steps to the house and finally broke contact, turned and ran up the steps and in through the backdoor.

He entered the mud room of the two-story farmhouse and found Jean and April in the hallway, kneeling on the floor to avoid the few stray rounds that had entered the house. Jean had her pistol out and was keeping watch on April. Cotton looked down at April and silently cursed himself for pushing her to the house instead of just shooting her. For all he knew, she was part of this obvious trap and he had just cornered himself and his daughter in the house with her.

In the melee, April completely lost the contact that had been in her left eye. She looked up at Cotton with one of her eyes crystal clear blue and the other milky white. She was scared. No, she was terrified. This woman was not the mastermind behind some grand plan. She was just a pawn.

For a moment, Cotton wondered if his humanity was slipping away. His summary judgement had been to execute her in the backyard and again in the hallway. Then he looked at his daughter and understood that it wasn't so simple. Perhaps he was becoming a monster, but he was becoming the monster his little girl would need to make it through this hell.

"Upstairs, now!" Cotton ordered.

Jean and April complied without question. April was sure that this man was still going to kill her, but perhaps she could buy herself the time she needed to make him understand why she had done what she did.

The two women went up the stairs first, and as they cleared the landing, Cotton heard footsteps coming up the rear stairway. Whoever it was began working the doorknob.

Cotton turned to the sound and brought his rifle up.

Click.

It wasn't an empty chamber. He knew the sound and feel of a bolt locking back, and he damn sure would have known if he was walking around the house with an empty rifle. No, it had jammed. Absurdly, he thought back to the last time he had thoroughly cleaned the DD M4. It had been a long time.

The rear door slammed open hard enough that it broke the glass in the window, and three men entered the hallway, weapons up.

Cotton released his grip on the rifle and his right hand dropped to the Safariland holster on his right hip. He drew the Glock 17 and brought the weapon up. His eyes caught the Trijicon red dot, but it wasn't necessary. Three men piling into a hallway... he couldn't miss.

The same speed shooting skills Cotton had

applied to his work in the yard with the M4 he now carried over to his pistol. He found the wall on the trigger, broke it and then fired faster than he ever had before. The Magpul GL9 magazine in his Glock held twenty-seven rounds. When he had first seen the polymer magazine upgrades, he'd thought they were a little silly. Who in the hell needed twenty-seven rounds in a pistol?

He did.

The hallway erupted into chaos. The men got off a couple of shots as they stumbled back the way they had come in, but it was too late. Cotton's hollow point rounds shredded them. He watched one man take three of them to the face and another had his throat torn out by the high pressure nine-millimeter ammunition. His blood sprayed the wall as his carotid artery spit his life force across the peeling paint.

"No!" The last man grunted as he fell through the doorway.

Cotton followed him down the steps and put a round in each of his legs. One wound spurted blood from the femoral artery. Cotton moved to the man, disarmed him, and then applied a CAT tourniquet with speed and precision.

The man looked up at him with a combination of

horror and confusion. Cotton stepped back and scanned his surroundings, then turned back to the man.

"Tell them to stop coming," he said coldly. "Or you all die."

Brian had sat in silence as Jorge drove them both north in his old Toyota truck. He wanted to say something, but wasn't sure what it should be.

"You been there? When you worked for the King?" Brian asked. "Up north, I mean."

"Yeah," Jorge replied. "I been there."

Brian knew little about the big man, aside from the fact that he had been straight with him since he showed up. Even though he didn't know Jorge's history, he could tell that he could handle himself.

"What's it like?" Brian inquired.

"Same as anywhere else," Jorge replied.

"What I'm trying to say, I suppose, is that I don't really know much about it. Or about the King."

"Not much to know," Jorge said. "He runs the show. That's all."

"I heard he killed the President."

Jorge shot Brian a dirty look and then put his eyes back on the road.

"Yeah, I heard the same thing."

"Shot him from a mile away or something."

"What is the point of this fucking conversation?" Jorge snapped.

"Just trying to... I don't know. Kill some time. It's at least an hour to Oatmeal and I don't really know much about you."

"Why do you need to know about me?" Jorge asked.

"I don't know. I just don't have many friends here."

"Well, we ain't gonna be friends," Jorge replied.

Brian let out a breath and relaxed into his seat.

"Whatever."

Jorge suddenly felt poorly. He wasn't sure why, but something about the young man got to him. It reminded him of being young in the Unit and feeling like he was woefully out of his depth. Sure, the other guys had mentored him, but he never really felt like he had a friend. The truth of it was, he never needed friends, but that did not mean that their absence went unnoticed.

"Look," Jorge said. "You know the world has changed. It's a different place now. You can't just... I don't know. Let people in. You know what I mean?"

"Sure," Brian said. "I get it. I just want to be on

the team. I guess I'm trying to figure out the best way to do that."

"You're doing it," Jorge said. "You passing on this info to the King helps maintain the balance. If what you said is true, there's someone real serious out there that may pose a threat to all of us. We need to get a handle on that."

"I get it," Brian said.

There was silence for a moment.

"Ask me a question," Jorge said.

"What?" Brian asked.

"Ask me a question. You want to get to know me, ask me something."

"Why did you take it?"

The question caught Jorge off-guard and he sent Brian a withering glance, but then relented. He let out a sigh.

"The vaccine," he said.

"Yeah," Brian said. "I mean, I know why I took it. Just didn't think anything of it. Back then I figured if the government and the CDC and all of them were pushing it, it must be fine."

Jorge laughed out loud and then caught himself.

"I'm not laughing at you," he said. "It's just the situation." He paused for a moment. "I was working in a job with Federal contracts. Word came down that anyone working on Federal contracts had to be vaccinated. I was kind of on the fence already, but I couldn't afford to lose my job. Back then, I had a wife and kids... so, yeah, I took it."

Brian nodded.

"No one thought it was going to turn into this," Jorge said, and he looked at Brian with his milky white eyes. "Not in a million years."

"I heard they're working on something to fix it," Brian said. "You hear anything about that?"

"I heard those rumors," Jorge said as he turned his eyes back to the road before him. "I hear a lot of things."

CHAPTER 5

COTTON CLOSED the door to the rear entrance and looked down at the two bodies on the floor. Both men were seriously kitted up. They wore Crye JPC plate carriers with a full complement of magazines and medical kits. They looked like they were pretty serious, but something was off.

The three men had piled into a small hallway with mostly mid-length barrel rifles and they panicked. It was hard to remember clearly, but Cotton was pretty sure one of them had even activated a white light.

Cotton went over the bodies, pulling off anything that might be useful to him. This included the magazines which would at least replenish the rounds he had dumped during the initial assault. He broke open the rifles and dropped the bolt carrier groups into his hand and pocketed them. There was already a spare in his ruck, but one never knew when a BCG might go south, even a good one. He also stripped the springs out of the Glock pistols. Those were the only parts he ever needed to change on the Austrian guns.

With this process finished, he dragged the bodies out the back door and left them on the steps. They would serve as a warning to anyone else who was dumb enough to come looking for their own demise.

Jean Wiley had been sitting on the floor of the second story house for several minutes watching April like a hawk. At first, Jean had kept the pistol trained on this woman who had one milky white eye, but she had since relaxed her grip a bit.

"I wasn't going to hurt you," April said quietly.

Jean did not reply. She heard footsteps coming up the stairs and turned to the open door that led out onto the second-floor landing. She saw her father rounding the corner. He looked old, older than she remembered. Jean wasn't sure why this jumped out at her in that exact moment, but it did. Perhaps it had become easy for her to always see him as her protector, as the tougher than nails SEAL who could do anything and beat anyone. The warrior who would take on all comers to protect his little girl and never be found wanting. It was easy to see him that way and forget that he was still just a man.

"This ain't over," Cotton said simply.

He walked across the room and took up a half-kneeling position at the window. From this vantage point, he could see the entire front yard area and all the way out to the road. No one would sneak up on him coming from that direction. If they tried to come through the rear door again or make entry from a side window, they would be fighting him from a dangerous position trying to come up the stairs.

Cotton turned to April.

"Talk!" He snapped. "Was your whole story bullshit?"

"No!" April countered, the panic coming back to her voice. "Not— not all of it! I was in that bunker with my Daddy for all that time, and when I came out, I did get picked up by Randall Eisler's men— "

"Who in the hell is Randall Eisler?" Cotton asked.

"He runs the community out at Cypress Mill."

"I'll make a wild guess that they're not an outlaw group of anti-vaxxers," Cotton said.

"They're— they're cannibals," April replied.

"Like you," Cotton said, driving the point home.

"I wasn't before," April said quietly, her lower lip quivering. "They made me take it after they found me. Said they couldn't trust me otherwise."

Cotton understood, and his posture relaxed. He was finally getting the big picture of what had really happened to April. He had heard about this kind of thing going down. Different groups of cannibals had gotten hold of vials of the original vaccine and used it as a conversion tool.

"They made you take the vaccine. Not to protect you but to guarantee compliance."

April nodded.

"I was so scared," she said. "I just didn't want to die. So, I took it."

"You were bait," Cotton realized as he thought back to how he had found her on the interstate. "Those men that were chasing you, you were working with them."

"They told me we were trying to lure out marauders and FPAR hold outs. They said we were trying to stop them from hurting innocent people caught out in the Meat Belt."

"And you believed that?" Cotton asked incredulously.

"No," April said, and shook her head. "I didn't

know what else to do. I was just trying to live another day."

"I assume you've eaten?" Cotton asked.

April met his eyes. She had known that a moment like this would come one day, a conversation with an unvaccinated person about her need to consume human flesh. She just hadn't expected it to happen this soon.

"Yes," she replied. "Last night. Before we left Cypress Mill."

"Then you'll be fine for a couple more days."

That was one benefit to having taken the vaccine and subsequently turning. Something about the consumption of human meat caused the cannibals to only have to feed every seventy-two hours, but they also seemed to have no hunger signals. When the time came that they needed to feed or risk their body breaking down and consuming itself, the urge hit like a hammer. Seventy-two hours was a fairly reliable estimate for most of them, but it could easily be more or less. If it was less, the result could be catastrophic.

When a cannibal slipped into that state of absolute hunger, it was something akin to a panic. They would become irrational and frenzied. That was how the attacks happened. There were theories about the neo-cortex shutting down and surrendering control to the brainstem, resulting in a more primal version of the human animal.

"Hey there!" A voice called from outside.

Cotton turned back to the window and saw a man standing a reasonable distance from the house. Close enough that they could hear him, but far enough away that at least a pistol round wouldn't hit him. He knew to stay at least that far away.

He looked to be in his early forties, maybe Cotton's age, but the end of the world had clearly been much kinder to him. His belly poked out from beneath his plate carrier and he wore the same sort of slick gear that the others had. This man even had a helmet on.

"Why don't we make a deal?" The man called out. "Know you got two girls in there. Just send one out and the other two of you can live. Pretty as you please. No hard feelings."

Cotton looked at April for a moment and then back out the window.

"No deals," Cotton said. "You ain't talkin' your way out of this. Make peace with your God."

Cotton slammed the window shut.

.   .   .

Harris Hawthorne walked back to the ravine and down the slope. He felt like he'd done a hell of a lot of walking that day. More than he cared for. He flashed back for a moment to his job as an insurance salesman, and in particular, his nice, comfy leather chair. Back then, he could sit in that leather chair all day watching Garand Thumb videos on YouTube and cursing the flat feet that had kept him from fulfilling his goal of becoming a Special Forces soldier.

That was what he should have been doing all along. Jumping out of airplanes and storming buildings. He was supposed to have been fighting evil, not helping people bundle their life insurance with fire and theft for fantastic savings.

Getting out to the range with the boys had at least been something. They were lucky to have access to a private range outside of Georgetown just north of Austin where they could do some good realistic training. A couple of them even had night vision and Harris had gotten to use it a couple of times. He even tried to make the case to his wife that getting some NODs would be a good investment for SHTF (shit hits the fan) type scenarios, but his arguments had fallen on deaf ears.

Then SHTF really came. Harris thought about

this for a moment. In a very real way, he had traded the boring, stale life he had been living for this new one. Losing that old life had also meant his wife leaving him. She wanted them to head for Houston, where most of the 'sane Texans' were gathering to hold on to some semblance of civilization.

The only problem with this idea was that Harris Hawthorne didn't want to hold on to civilization. He liked the new world. He liked driving around in his Toyota pickup with the boys, scavenging for supplies and then getting drunk around the campfire at night telling war stories.

He'd even shot a few people in the very beginning. Maybe they had it coming and maybe they didn't, but they had been in the wrong place at the wrong time. Just bad luck is all. It also didn't hurt that him and the boys needed things to maintain the lifestyle they had become accustomed to, and if you had those things and weren't willing to part with them peaceably, well... that was why they had the law of the jungle. The strong survive.

So, the wife went to live with her mother in Houston. She and Harris acted like they were just taking a break, even talked about "seeing each other soon" but they both knew that wasn't true. They wanted different things. They wanted to live in different worlds.

Then things changed again. Harris and the boys went to one of the FEMA camps to get the poke. At first, some of the boys didn't like the idea, but all the leaflets said, "No questions asked." More and more, it didn't seem like it was some elaborate trap to hunt down marauders or FPAR. That, and the rising lethality of the virus, finally tipped the scales, and they all opted in. It would be a hell of a thing to lose this new life he was building because he got some superbug.

At first, everything seemed fine. They all knew it took a while for the poke to have an effect. No one quite understood why it happened like that, but it was at least a few months before your eyes changed enough for anyone to notice. That was how so much of the population could get vaccinated before they knew about the actual side effects.

Long before their own eyes changed, Harris and the boys started hearing the stories. In the beginning, they laughed at it. Cannibals. Yeah, right. The vaccine was turning people into cannibals. Even now Harris wondered how many people, maybe how many millions, took the vaccine even after those stories started coming out just because it sounded so crazy.

Then their eyes changed. Then the hunger came and along with that was panic. The other part of the story was that after seventy-four hours, starvation sets in. You had maybe another day after that until you began consuming yourself from the inside.

Jesus, Harris had thought to himself. *That's a hell of a way to go.*

For some reason, though, that made sense to him. It made sense that folks who'd gone cannibal would eventually consume themselves. That understanding made things more real. It helped him accept his role in this new world.

He would become a hunter of men.

That role had then brought them to this house.

Something about the house pulled people in. Maybe it was how it stood like a beacon just off this road that so many people had traveled down. Maybe it was the fact that it was the only one for miles. Folks just had a tendency to come to it looking for food or shelter.

In that way, it had become a trap.

Harris and the boys still did all the typical things when it came to stocking up on needed supplies, and those supplies could still frequently be found in the surrounding towns and cities. The countryside hadn't been ransacked the way you always saw in apocalypse movies. There was plenty to go around because there just weren't that many people out looking for it.

When it came to the one thing they truly needed though, human flesh, that was something they had to procure on their own. Not only that, but setting traps like this one worked best for drawing people in.

Except this time was different. Whoever the hell that guy was in the house, he had balls the size of, well... Texas. At the bottom of the ravine, Harris found his second in command, Bob Wilson. Bob had been a lawyer in Austin. He was kind of a big deal too; you couldn't drive down any length of Interstate Thirty-Five without seeing one of his billboards.

Now Bob was different. Harris had noticed something about the man's eyes had changed, beyond their milky hue. They were colder. Harris had accepted his lot in the new world, but he hadn't ever gotten used to the idea that they now ate other human beings to survive. Not that he had a significant problem with it, but he also didn't necessarily like it.

Bob liked it.

"Didn't sound like that went well," Bob said flatly.

"No," Harris replied. "I can't say that it did."

"So, what's the play?"

Harris looked around at the other men. They were all waiting for him to say something, to make a decision. They followed him because, so far, he'd been right at every turn. Of course, except for the part where he made a decision that turned them all into cannibals, but no one gets it right every time. They understood that.

"I don't like it," Harris said. "The way he's acting, and he already smoked five of the boys."

"We've still got two dozen in the ranks," Bob countered.

"True, true," Harris replied. "But the whole point of this ruse is to provide sustenance. If he ends up putting half of the boys in the ground, it kind of defeats the point, don't it?"

"We bum rush the house," Bob said. "He can't get all of us."

"This guy... seems like he might be special forces or something. You heard how fast he was shooting out back of the house."

"Yeah," Bob acquiesced. "That was pretty damn fast, and he was hitting his targets."

"He's got an elevated position and possibly two more guns with him if the girls can shoot. It's a bad play."

Bob stared at his commander. Harris could read his eyes.

"No," Harris said simply.

"It was gonna happen sometime," Bob said. "You know it and I know it. I get that you want us to be Treaty Members and we still will be—"

"Under Randall Eisler!" Harris snapped.

Bob looked at where the men were gathered, each one listening intently to the conversation. He waved Harris away from the group, just out of earshot.

"I get it," Bob said. "I do. Right now, you run the show. We do our own thing and it's been great; it really has. But can we keep this up forever? I mean, we've been damn lucky no one has had a medical issue or needed something we can't provide. We throw in with Randall Eisler and we're golden. We'd be full treaty members and no one's gonna say 'boo' to us."

"But we're not our own men anymore."

"I don't know about that," Bob said. "Randall Eisler's got those hunting parties that go out. We could get on with him and have a gig like that. We're still our own men, we've just got insurance."

Harris laughed at the obvious reference to his past as an insurance salesman.

"Okay," Harris said. "What do you propose?"

"Send a couple guys out to Cypress Mill with our situation and ask for some backup. They'll come back with a couple dozen hitters and some machine guns and we'll bulldoze this motherfucker."

Harris thought about it for a moment and then nodded.

"Okay," Harris said. "I know you're right."

"We also have to keep Houston in mind," Bob followed up.

"How do you mean?"

"They're growing," Bob said. "We've seen two government vehicles out here in the past two weeks. We know Randall Eisler and The King have a direct line to them. I ain't ever living in one of those damn cities, but if the time comes that they start looking to consolidate territory, I want to know as much as I can about their intentions and capabilities."

Cotton sat by the window waiting for some response, for the pot belly man in his plate carrier and helmet to come back out, but he never did. The former SEAL looked down at his watch and saw that it was only half past noon. That whole thing had happened so fast.

Neither Jean nor April had said a word. They only sat in silence.

"There's something I don't understand," Jean said, directing the words at April. "Last night when I found you out there getting ready to take your life."

"What?" Cotton asked, clearly surprised.

"If you already knew everything that had happened, why were you acting like you didn't?" Jean asked.

"It wasn't that," April said. "I thought it was a way out of hurting you."

Cotton wasn't sure how to respond to that. He knew it would be safer to just throw this woman to the wolves or even to end her himself. It would be safer for him and for his daughter. Still, that wasn't who he was. It wasn't who he wanted Jean to be.

"We can get you somewhere," Cotton said. "Somewhere you've got a chance. If you need us to."

April nodded her thanks.

"There's a community west of here. A place I heard about," April said.

"For your kind?" Cotton asked.

"For Gatherers."

Cotton shook his head.

"That won't last. You must know that."

Gatherers was the slang name for cannibals who only consumed those they found who had already expired naturally. For the moment it was a viable tactic, but as Cotton had said, it would only be so long before the Gatherers had to become Hunters.

"For now, it's all I've got," April pleaded. "If the rumors are true about the second vaccine, maybe I only have to hold on a little longer."

"Yeah," Cotton laughed. "Because the first one worked out so well."

"Maybe they got it right this time!" April countered. "Maybe it can make me human again."

"Could also just be talk," Cotton said. "I haven't seen any leaflets falling from the sky about it, not like the first time."

Jean gave her father a dirty look, and he relented. Cotton understood. Even if this idea of a second vaccine that could reverse what the first had done wasn't true, at least it was giving April hope. If only for a short while.

"Okay," Cotton said. "We'll get you there."

"Thank you," April said.

"That's assuming we make it out of this damn house in one piece," Cotton went on.

Cotton worked his way to a standing position. He wanted to ignore the fact that every joint in his body hurt, but that was getting harder and harder to do. He pulled the tab on his Ferro Concepts Slingster to bring the rifle closer to his body. This kept it secured to him so that his hands would be free. If he needed to, he could grab the tab on the sling to release it and bring his weapon up in a matter of seconds.

The house was dead quiet. That was good, because if any of these amateurs tried to make entry, he was likely to hear them coming a mile away.

Back in the rear hallway, he found the weapons and gear he'd stripped off the dead men and retrieved their carbines. One was a longer 14.5" barrel while the other was a shorty with a 10.3" barrel. Apparently, one of them had thought he was a Close Quarters Battle expert with that short barrel. Cotton had disabused him of that notion, and it cost the man his life. In this new world, death was often the penalty for arrogance.

He also gathered up some magazines and stuffed them into his pockets. At a glance, he saw they were loaded up with 62 grain green tips. That would be enough to stop whatever came at them. They weren't in the same class as his 77 grain hollow points, but they would do just fine all the same.

Cotton hit the top of the stairs and entered the room. He sat on the floor and broke open the longer barrel AR. He reached back into his front pocket and retrieved one of the bolt carrier groups he had earlier removed from the rifle and dropped it back in. From there, he closed the rifle back up and repeated the same process on the short barrel. Once he finished with this, he loaded a magazine into each one and handed the short barrel to his daughter.

The surprise in her eyes was clear.

"It's time," Cotton said and nodded his head, encouraging her to take it.

Jean had been carrying the Hellcat pistol for nearly a year at that point, all the way back to the little cabin in West Virginia. He'd let her carry it because he knew she needed to be able to defend herself if, for some reason, he wasn't around. Unfortunately, that had proven to be the case on three separate occasions while they were on the road.

Even after that, he'd been resistant to the idea of putting a carbine in her hand, even something like the shorty MK18 she was now holding. It wasn't because he thought she couldn't handle it. It was because he couldn't let go of the idea that she was just a girl, and girls like her shouldn't be fighting for their lives. She should be going to school and making friends, wearing a unicorn backpack and spending weekends at the mall.

Those things were all a big part of the reason Cotton had done what he had in the military. His actions overseas should have been money in the bank, an investment in his daughter's future.

Instead, she now sat across from him on the floor of this house in the middle of nowhere, function-checking her rifle.

Cotton turned his attention to April. He looked at her for a moment and held out the second rifle.

She reached out for it but he kept his grip and locked eyes with her.

"I'm trusting you," he said. "That means something."

"I won't let you down," April said.

Cotton released his grip and she took the weapon.

"You know how to use it, right?" Cotton asked.

April nodded.

"Just to review," Cotton said with a hint of a smile as he touched the magazine release. "This is not the trigger."

"Ha ha," April said and chambered a round.

CHAPTER 6

"We're here," Jorge said as he elbowed Brian and rolled the Toyota to a stop.

Brian opened his eyes and rubbed away the sleep. He didn't even remember passing out, but it shouldn't have been much of a surprise, considering he hadn't slept the night before.

"Damn," Brian said quietly as he sat up in his seat. "These guys are serious."

They parked the Toyota on Farm Road 243, the main entry point to Oatmeal, Texas.

Two big rigs sat jackknifed on the road, never to be moved again. It was much like the setup they had at Cypress Mill, but on steroids. Mounted atop the trailers were two fifty-caliber machine-gun nests, and it looked like they even had some rocket launchers set up. Jorge had never thought this was all to protect the community from marauders. No, it seemed to him like the King was expecting something bigger. He just didn't know what that was.

Behind the big rigs, they could see what looked like miles of concertina wire strung out with clearly visible checkpoints and roving patrols. Everything was uniform and clearly organized.

"They'll come out to meet us," Jorge said, keeping his eyes on the road as the engine idled. "Don't say shit."

Brian nodded his understanding, and as if on cue, a man dressed in full military gear and toting a carbine walked through the opening between the two big rigs and headed toward them.

"Shut it off!" The sentry shouted, pointing a finger at the truck.

Jorge killed the engine, and Brian watched the big man's hand slide between the seat and the console. There was a gun there. What was he planning on doing?

The sentry approached the driver's side window of the Toyota but kept a reasonable distance. He brought the short rifle up to the low ready. Brian looked past him and saw one of the fifty cals swivel toward them.

"State your business," the sentry said firmly.

"I'm here to see the King," Jorge said matter-of-factly. "Randall Eisler sent me."

The sentry keyed a radio on his vest and spoke into it. He waited for a moment until it crackled to life and he received a response.

"You have to leave your weapons at the gate," the sentry ordered. "But he says you can come in."

"Roger that," Jorge nodded, and his right hand slid back from the space between the seat and the console.

The sentry waved them forward and Jorge started the engine and pulled up to the repurposed cattle gate that blocked off the entrance between the two semis. Another sentry approached with what looked like a military duffel bag.

"Weapons, unloaded," the sentry said.

Jorge reached back down between the seat and the console and retrieved his Colt 1911. He dropped the magazine and then locked the slide back, catching the ejected round mid-air.

"Pretty slick," the sentry said with a smile as he took the firearm and carefully set it into the bag. "How long it take you to learn that?"

"Only a few weeks. Every night. Sitting on my couch watching Twenty-Four," Jorge replied.

The sentry laughed as Brian passed over the two carbines that had been on the floorboard behind the front seats.

"Fair enough," the sentry replied as another man opened the cattle gate. "Check in at the third house on the left. They'll get you taken care of."

"Will do," Jorge replied, and pulled through the gate.

"Holy shit," Brian said, and sat up in his seat.

"Yeah," Jorge replied. "Holy shit."

The town was not what Brian had expected. In his mind's eye, he had envisioned something similar to Cypress Mill, which looked more like a dilapidated boy's club/ outpost at the end of the world than anywhere a civilized person might live. This place was different.

The mark of the apocalypse was on the town, no doubt about it, but clearly they were working hard to maintain things as best they could. People walked down the street having conversations. A mail truck was making the rounds and there were even shops open. It was the closest thing Brian had seen to civilization in a long time.

"It's like nothing ever happened," Brian said in disbelief.

"Well, I wouldn't go quite that far," Jorge replied.

"But yeah, it's a far cry from anything else you'll find in the Texas Meat Belt."

"How do they keep it like this?" Brian asked. "I mean, it's so civilized."

Jorge rounded a corner and pulled to a stop in front of an old courthouse. This was where Brian received the answer to his question.

"That's how," Jorge replied.

On the landing of the courthouse were some makeshift stocks straight out of the old west or medieval times. In them, a man was locked with his head and arms protruding through the front. He had clearly been beaten and where his hands should have been were only bloody, cauterized stumps. A neatly lettered sign was posted beside him that read simply: "I am a thief."

"Jesus," Brian gasped.

"Mind your Ps and Qs," Jorge said, "and you won't have to worry about that."

Brian seemed transfixed by the man in the stocks.

"Hey!" Jorge snapped, getting his attention. "Get your head in the game!"

"Right," Brian said quickly and got out of the truck. "Sorry."

"Anyway, we ain't going there yet. We've got to check-in first."

Jorge walked a block down and stopped at a small blue house set a little further back from the street than the others. He walked down the small path to the front door and was almost to it when it opened before him.

A woman stood in the doorway. Grey strands streaked her long black hair and her green eyes locked on Jorge. Brian noted she wore a gun on her hip and the finish had worn off of it. Either she or someone else had been using that firearm quite a bit.

"Well," she said, "look what the cat dragged in."

"Hey, Sheila," Jorge said sheepishly.

"Hey?" She mocked. "Wow! That's really great Jorge."

Jorge looked back at Brian and then to her.

"Can we take this inside?" He asked.

"Hold out your hand," Sheila ordered.

Jorge looked scared.

"Why?"

"Don't be an idiot," she snapped and held up a hand stamp. "What did you think I was going to do, stab you?"

"Like it would be the first time," Jorge shot back.

"Well, we are cannibals, honey," she said with a

smile and stamped his hand. "Hey you, shit for brains."

Brian looked around.

"Yes, you!" Sheila pressed.

Brian stepped forward and Sheila grabbed his wrist and stamped his hand.

"That'll keep you two idiots out of trouble for twenty-four hours," Sheila said. "Now get the hell off my lawn."

Jorge didn't bother saying anything, and instead turned and led Brian away.

"That seemed like it went really well. I think she likes you a lot," Brian said. "She seems really nice."

"Shut up."

"Just don't do anything stupid and we'll be fine," Jorge said to Brian as they stood in the hallway outside of what used to be the mayor's office. "Just say what you saw. Nothing more."

"Got it," Brian said.

"No, listen," Jorge said, and turned to the young man. "That last part is important. Nothing more. This guy... he reads people and he'll get things out of you that you didn't even know were there."

"I get it," Brian said, clearly confused by Jorge's

demand.

As if on cue, the door opened and a tall, thin man with close cropped hair stepped out. He looked at Jorge for a moment and then smiled.

"Long time no see," he said and extended his hand.

Jorge shook it and nodded.

"Good to see you, Wilson," Jorge lied.

"You caught him in a good mood," Wilson said. "He just got to cut someone's hands off."

It was not a joke, and both Jorge and Brian knew it was a reference to the man outside in stocks.

Wilson waved the two in, and they crossed the threshold into the large office. Beside the window stood a man in a clean and pressed business suit. Despite the attire, it was clear he had no history as a businessman. He was five foot ten and built like a bulldog with the absence of a neck to match. Brian saw he was wearing an expensive Rolex, but this extravagancy was in stark contrast to the tattoos on his hands and fingers.

He turned to the two men and stared at them sternly for a moment. Then his face broke out into a broad grin.

"Gotta say Hermano, I was starting to think I'd never see you again!" Roland Reese said as he walked across the room with surprising speed and embraced Jorge in a big bear hug that nearly knocked the much taller man off his feet.

Jorge returned the embrace, and this time it was sincere.

Roland stepped back and straightened his tie.

"You know how it is," Jorge replied with a shrug. "Had to move on. Had my reasons."

"Maybe someday you'll enlighten me," Roland said. "As to what those reasons were." Roland turned his attention to Brian. "I assume this is the young man I was called about?"

"This is Brian," Jorge said. "He has something to tell you."

Cotton had moved through the house as stealthily as possible and locked all the doors and windows and drawn the curtains. The structure was by no means secure, but they could at least move around and would have some additional warning if anyone tried to make entry.

They stayed on the top floor, as anyone trying to get in would have a hell of a time moving up the stairs with Cotton chucking tear gas at them and firing a flurry of 5.56 rounds. He'd been holding onto the large canisters of "Clear Out" tear gas, but this seemed as good a time as any to use them.

He hadn't been cornered like this before. The whole time they were on the road, and all the fights he'd been in, there was always a way out. He made sure of that in advance, but not this time. He'd walked right into what should have been an obvious trap. Not only that, but he'd also walked into a trap the other night rescuing April. That time, it was just a trap that hadn't worked.

He knew it was nothing to beat himself up about. It was just another teachable moment. It was another lesson to learn, so long as he could make it out of this in one piece. Even if they had to hold out for the rest of the day, he knew what the endgame would be. Once night fell, he'd go NODs down and take the fight to them, and they would not like it.

There was a decent chance at least some of these guys would also have night vision based on how they were kitted up, but that didn't mean they knew how to use it. Most folks who got night vision all did the same thing. They went to the range in the dark and shot at targets. Very few understood the importance of going out and walking, running, negotiating obstacles and fighting in night vision. That was the hard part, not the shooting.

Cotton walked back into the bedroom they had taken over as their headquarters. Jean had fallen asleep in an easy chair in the corner with her rifle cradled in her arms. Cotton smiled at that. He knew it meant a lot to her that he had given her the weapon. In this strange new world, that was just as much a rite of passage as getting your first car or going to prom.

April sat on the floor where he had left her. She looked up at Cotton as he entered. He turned to the old wooden chair in the corner. It appeared to be made by hand, and while the paint was peeling here and there, it seemed as if it would be plenty comfortable compared to the hardwood floor.

"You can sit in that chair if you like," Cotton said.

He crossed the room and sat down on an old trunk across from the chair. April got up, feeling for the first time the effect of the adrenaline that had been coursing through her veins and the past two hours of sitting in one position. She sat down in the chair and let out a breath.

Cotton thought for a moment about unslinging his rifle, but then decided against it. Instead, he pulled back the charging handle to confirm that there was still a round in the chamber and then leaned back against the wall. He had already known there was a round in the chamber, because there always was, but it was his version of being superstitious.

"This place you want to go to," Cotton said. "You know where it is?"

"I heard the men talking about it at Cypress Mill. They have some kind of deal with the King, the Gatherers do. That's why he lets them be. Said it was just outside a town called Tow, over by the Colorado River. If you've got a map, it shouldn't be hard to find."

"Okay," Cotton replied. "Like I said, we'll get you there."

April stared into Cotton's eyes for a moment.

"Mind if I ask you something?" April asked. "It's kinda private."

"I don't mind."

"Why didn't you take it?"

"The vaccine?" Cotton asked. "In the beginning, I wasn't sure if I was going to or not. I'd already had the government shoot me up with one experimental vaccine. When I went into the Navy in 2001, I was one of the last to get the anthrax vaccine. Later on, I found out that thing messed a lot of people up, but still I was open to the new one. The virus seemed like it was only picking up speed."

"What changed your mind?"

"They started trying to force people to take it. First, there were a bunch of crazy regulations about how you had to have it to go in restaurants and all that. I didn't care too much about that. Then the Feds released a date by which you would have to upload your vaccine documents to maintain a bank account. For me, that's when I knew I wasn't going to take it. I knew something was wrong."

"You think they knew?" April asked. "What it was going to do? What it would turn people into?"

Cotton shrugged.

"I'm no scientist and I sure ain't no doctor. I'm good at a few things and none of them have anything to do with understanding vaccines and viruses." Cotton looked to his daughter sleeping in the easy chair and smiled. "Only thing I care about is getting her someplace where she has a chance."

"I want to help," April said. "However I can."

"You think you're ready to fight?" Cotton asked. "If it comes to that?"

"I can fight," April said. "I keep thinking... I don't know. Maybe I should have fought back when they tried to put this poison in me. Maybe it would have been better to die than to be this... thing."

"What's done is done," Cotton said. "Fastest way

to get your ticket punched out here is to waste time regretting what you should or shouldn't have done. You have to be one hundred percent focused on survival."

Ralph hadn't signed up for this. What he had done was make the crucial mistake of telling the truth. Specifically, that he had a background in breaking and entering, and maybe even did a little time for it in juvie. This was before he turned his life around and became the best damn used car salesman ever to hit Round Rock, Texas.

Milton, on the other hand, had committed no such crime. He'd just been unlucky enough to be the poor son of a bitch standing next to Ralph when Harris 'volunteered' the two of them to get into the farmhouse. Now Milton stood beside the house with his AR scanning their surroundings as Ralph jimmied the cheap lock on the first-floor window.

"Okay," Ralph said. "You know the drill."

They were actually pretty good at this by now. Like most of the boys before the collapse, Milton had spent most of his downtime drinking beers and watching YouTube videos about Close Quarters Battle and other military subjects. It had always been for fun, kind of a live action role playing thing. Never in a million years had he thought he'd actually use any of this stuff in real life.

Milton stepped back and short stocked the rifle over his shoulder, keeping the Aimpoint red dot centered on the window as Ralph set his own rifle down and lifted the window frame. If someone popped out from inside, they'd get a greeting from Milton, 5.56 style.

Ralph wasn't as confident. He'd been there for the slaughter behind the house, and that's exactly what he thought it was: a slaughter. That so-and-so had taken them all out like they were nothing, and he shot so fast! He'd never seen anything like it, not even on Instagram. He tried to tell Harris that this guy was some kind of special forces soldier and they should maybe leave him be, but his advice fell on deaf ears.

Privately, Ralph thought Harris was developing a bit of a god complex, and his right-hand man, Bob, wasn't helping matters.

Ralph parted the curtains and poked his head in the window. He looked around and surveyed the living room. No one seemed to be around, so he gave a wave back to Milton and shimmied the rest of the way in, quietly crawling onto the threadbare carpet.

He turned and reached back out the window where Milton handed him his AR-15.

The idea was to catch this man by surprise and take him by force. The thing that made Ralph uncomfortable about this whole idea was that he knew Harris had sent a runner to Randall Eisler for re-enforcements. That meant Harris thought it was possible they would fail.

He at least felt a little better about having Milton at his back. The much bigger man had been in the Army (albeit as a truck driver) but more importantly, he'd actually fought in the UFC. Considering they were going into a potential close combat situation, this seemed like a good background to have.

Ralph stayed close to the wall as Milton slipped in the window and then reached back out to retrieve his own rifle that he had lain against the exterior wall.

The location of the living room in the house caused it to be fairly dark, even in the afternoon, as not much natural light was making it in with all the curtains drawn. That wasn't too much of a problem, as they all knew the floorpan of this house like the backs of their hands. They knew the layout because it was a trap that had worked many times before.

Ralph thought about that for a moment, about

the idea that they used this house to trap other people for consumption. He only let that thought in for a moment and then pushed it out again. It was better not to think about it. He wasn't like that ghoul, Bob. He didn't enjoy any of this. It was just about survival.

Two doors led out of the living room, one to the kitchen and one to a hallway. In the hallway was a staircase that would take them to the second floor. It was a fairly logical assumption that this man would be on the second floor. No one would be dumb enough to hide in the kitchen.

Ralph held up his hand and waved to Milton to follow him to the staircase.

The two men moved quietly through the door and into the hallway. Light crept in from the second-floor windows, so they could clearly see what lay ahead of them. They moved to the stairway. This was it. Ralph could feel his heart pounding in his ears and he tightened his grip on the rifle as he quietly flicked the selector switch on his AR from 'safe' to 'semi.' He could feel the weight of his pistol on his hip and suddenly couldn't remember if he had chambered a round. Of course he had! He must have. Did he?

Amid this mental freak out, Ralph felt Milton's

hand on his shoulder. He stopped and looked up.

It was a girl. She was tall but she was young. She stood at the top of the stairs, watching them. Ralph suddenly thought of his sister. She wasn't young like that anymore, but he remembered when she was. He also remembered when he'd whip anyone that looked at her sideways. What had happened to him? What in the hell was he doing?

The little girl stood there in the semi-darkness, staring at them. Then her eyes moved. What was she looking at?

She was looking at something behind them.

Cotton Wiley emerged from the darkness with his Winkler fixed blade knife at the ready, but he didn't need to strike. Instead, he put his hand over Milton's mouth, tripped the big man and let him fall back onto the blade. There was an audible hiss as it penetrated his right lung and Cotton turned quickly and used Milton's own momentum to slam him into the wall.

"No!" Ralph shouted.

Ralph brought up his AR, but then something horrible happened.

Cotton Wiley took it away from him. How in the hell had he done that? Ralph had secured the weapon to him. Then he realized in a sickening instant that this man was so fast he had actually disconnected Ralph's sling from the forward Quick Detach point.

Cotton threw the rifle into the living room and lunged forward. He slipped his hands between Ralph's raised arms, wrapped them around the back of his head and threw the hardest flying knee of his life into the would-be killer's face.

This man was trying to kill his little girl. That was all Cotton needed to know.

Ralph's head whipped back as Cotton released it and blood spurted from his broken nose. His body slammed into the floor with an audible "thud." He didn't move after that.

By now Milton had stumbled back to his feet, Cotton's knife still protruding from his back. Milton either didn't realize what had happened or he didn't care as he drew his pistol and brought the red dot sight up to his field of view.

Cotton took this weapon away as well. He just grabbed the slide, ripped the pistol out of the man's hand with a downward twist, and threw it in the living room with Ralph's rifle. Next, Cotton threw a palm strike at Milton's face. The big man saw stars and dropped to a single knee.

Opportunity had presented itself. Cotton

grabbed the handle of his fixed blade, pulled it back out of Milton's ribs, and went to work. He threw strike after strike, after strike, burying the blade repeatedly until Milton was flat on the floor and Cotton could feel the steel blade grinding against bone.

After what felt like a furious eternity, Cotton dropped the knife and brought his carbine up. The rifle had been secured to his body with the Slingster the whole time, and now he readied himself for the assault force that must be coming.

He held the EOTech reticle on the hallway door and slowed his breathing down as he waited. His thumb hovered next to the tail cap button of the Surefire, ready to blind whoever was stupid enough to be the first man in the door.

Nothing. They didn't come. What in the hell were they playing at? Why just waste these men on a fool's errand?

Because they have no idea what they're doing, he thought to himself.

Harris stood on the old country road that led from the house out to the connecting single lane roads that would take a person further and further from the main route. He slid his foot around in the gravel and smiled. Whoever this guy was, even if he held them off, once night fell, it would be a different story. With their night vision capabilities, he wouldn't stand a chance.

Bob walked up the road from the house toward Harris, shaking his head.

"I didn't hear nothing," Harris said.

If Ralph and Milton were going to fail, he would have expected to hear some gunfire.

"I think it went down quiet," Bob said. "Either way, it's been forty-five minutes and they haven't come back. I don't think they're going to."

"Son-of-a-bitch!" Harris snapped.

The two men turned to the sound of feet slapping the gravel as another man ran toward them. It was Denny, a younger (and admittedly excitable) member of the group who was a recent addition from just a few months prior.

Bob held up a hand to slow him down.

"What's up Denny?"

"I saw one!" Denny said breathlessly.

"Saw one what?" Harris pressed, more than moderately annoyed by the intrusion. He was pretty sure that young Denny should be standing watch over by the eastern field.

Denny made the sign of the cross over his forehead.

"Bullshit," Harris snapped. "No one's seen one of those whack jobs for months."

"I saw three," Denny clarified. "Standing in the field. Just watching me."

"And you didn't get a shot off?" Harris asked incredulously.

"I— I— " Denny stuttered.

"It's fine," Bob said, putting a hand on the young man's shoulder. "But you have to be straight with us. You're sure it was them? Crosses and everything?"

"I'm sure," Denny insisted. "And you told me! You said it! Where there's one, there's ten."

"I did say that," Bob nodded and then looked at Harris. "We have to take this seriously."

"What do you mean?" Harris asked.

"We have to leave," Bob said simply.

Harris held his tongue, then turned to Denny.

"Run on back to the camp. Tell them to hold fast and that we may have company."

Denny looked to Bob.

"You don't look at him!" Harris snapped. "I still run this group!"

"Yes, sir!" Denny replied.

Without another word, Denny turned and ran back down the gravel road the way he had come.

"You're right, you know," Bob said. "You do run this group, and I support you in that role."

"Good," Harris said with a nod.

"Because you usually make the right decision," Bob went on. "But this doesn't feel like that."

"What are you saying?" Harris inquired.

"Just think it over," Bob said. "If it really is them, you know what I said was true. Where there's one, there's ten, and they play for keeps."

"So do I."

Roland Reese, otherwise known as the King of the Texas Meat Belt, sat quietly at his desk with his hands folded in front of him as he listened to young Brian's tale. He did not like what he was hearing. There was a reason he had put a treaty in place and appointed Treaty Members to uphold it.

Men could not be relied upon to govern themselves and not act like total savages. Roland wished that wasn't the case, but it was. He understood that simple truth when the President died. He knew someone would have to step in to fill that void, at least in central Texas.

After that shot, after the man in charge and his lackeys were gone, the real collapse started. Roland had to move fast, so he used his newfound reputation as the man who had killed the President, to build a following. It only took six months to establish the treaty as law and to enforce it viciously enough that everyone fell in line. Even folks he'd never met.

Folks like Randall Eisler. Roland figured that Randall Eisler could have held out just fine on his own. The man had a very interesting background as a logistics manager for a lumberyard as well as military experience, and those same skills had transferred over nicely to building his little community out in Cypress Mill. It also didn't hurt that people seemed to like Randall Eisler. They wanted to follow him.

Based on Roland's reputation alone, Randall Eisler had sent a courier to Oatmeal, volunteering to become a Treaty Member and bring his folks along with him. That had been a big deal. That, in Roland Reese's humble opinion, was where society needed to go. Ruling with brutality had a finite timeline. No, if you wanted your empire to last, you needed to give people something to believe in, something to stand for.

That was what The Treaty represented. This was what the future of America would look like.

Thus, what sounded like one man roaming around out there doing whatever the hell he pleased, was a problem. Not only that, but he was a very capable man. A man who could seriously disrupt the balance Roland had worked so hard to strike in central Texas.

Having finished his story, Brian fell silent.

"And, you're sure?" Roland asked. "You're sure that there was no one else? That this man was acting alone?"

A thin coat of sweat covered Brian's brow. Roland could see that the young man was terrified. He slid back in his rolling chair and reached under his desk. Brian reflexively pulled back, clearly expecting a gun to come out. Roland held up a hand and smiled. He cracked the small dorm fridge beneath the desk and pulled out two cans of Lone Star Beer. He tossed one to Jorge and handed the other to Brian.

"Go along to get along, right?" Roland asked.

"Yes, sir," Brian said.

He felt the can was cold in his hand. He hadn't touched a can of cold beer in how long he couldn't remember.

"We're building something here, Brian," Roland said, and leaned back in his chair. "You can probably see that just by walking the streets outside, right?" Roland looked at Jorge. "How about you, old friend? Can you see it?"

"I see it," Jorge nodded.

"But?" Roland asked and leaned forward.

Jorge paused for a moment and Roland made the "give it to me" sign with his hands.

"Come on," Jorge said with a shrug. "What do you want me to say? You know me."

"The stocks, right?" Roland asked.

"It's just not my style," Jorge said, and then looked to Brian. "Wait in the hall."

Brian looked to Roland, who nodded his approval. Jorge noted this.

The door closed behind the young man.

Jorge turned to Roland.

"I don't want to undermine your authority," Jorge said. "That's why I sent him out."

Roland's instinct was to be angry. As if this man even had the ability to undermine him, but he also understood that Jorge's heart was in the right place.

"You can't go back, you know," Roland said as he fished another beer out of the fridge and cracked it open. "Country's as cooked as a

Christmas turkey. Ain't ever going back to the way it was."

"I know."

"So, what's the problem, then? You think these people are gonna do right just because we ask?"

"Never know if you don't ask," Jorge countered. "If you just go around cuttin' their freaking hands off."

Roland locked eyes with the much bigger man for a moment and then relented.

"That may have been an... overreaction," Roland acquiesced. "But what's done is done."

"That's what everyone keeps telling me."

"Did it ever occur to you, in your infinite fucking wisdom, that if you'd been around, maybe that sorry son-of-a-bitch out in front wouldn't have gotten his hands cut off?"

Jorge took another pull off of his Lone Star beer and then set it down on the desk.

"Roland, this is a classic 'run out the clock' type of scenario for me. I'm just trying to do my portion and get by until the Big Man calls me home."

"Until you die. You just want to spin your wheels until you die."

"That's about the size of it," Jorge agreed. "And if I can get a cold beer once in a while, all the better."

"You know—"

The main door to the office opened and interrupted Roland Reese. Wilson walked in, holding a satellite phone.

"What is it?" Roland asked.

"Got a call from Randall Eisler," Wilson said. "Says he thinks some group of marauders might have our mystery man cornered in a farmhouse north of Round Rock."

This caught Jorge's attention as well.

"The guy from last night?" Jorge asked.

"They think it has to be him," Wilson confirmed. "This marauder captain relayed that this guy already smoked six of their crew. He's asking Randall Eisler to send backup."

"Really?" Roland asked and rubbed his chin for a moment. He turned to Jorge. "What do you say? Feel like taking a road trip?"

"Why me?" Jorge asked. "You've got plenty of guys that could do this."

"Not like you," Roland said pointedly. "Look, do this one thing for me. Just this one thing and if you still want out, I'll never bring it up again."

Jorge thought about it for a moment and then nodded.

"But I'm finishing this beer first."

CHAPTER 7

RALPH OPENED his eyes and blinked a few times to refocus his vision. Once this process was finished, he could clearly see the man sitting across from him. Cotton Wiley looked like a literal messenger of death. He glared at Ralph from behind steel-blue eyes.

Ralph could feel that his hands were bound to the chair and the middle of his face hurt something awful. If he even had something resembling a nose left, it was no doubt destroyed.

Standing behind his adversary were two women, or, to be more specific, a woman and a young girl. Something about the girl was unnerving, almost as if the eyes that rested in her face were older than her years. She wasn't looking at Ralph; she was looking through him. She had that thousand-yard stare you always heard about in war movies. After a moment, he recognized she was the one who had been standing at the top of the stairs.

"Make no mistake," Cotton said, "You are going to die. What you say next will determine the duration and the method of that outcome, but not the outcome itself."

It wasn't a bluff. Ralph knew this. He could tell just by looking at Cotton. This was not a man prone to lies.

"I was just— I was just—"

"Don't say you were following orders," Cotton said. "That hasn't worked out well for folks in the past, and it won't go any better for you."

Ralph stopped himself from commenting further and just nodded his understanding.

"How many in your party?" Cotton asked.

"About thirty," Ralph said, and then corrected himself. "Well, less now."

"What capabilities do you have?"

"AR platforms and pistols on everyone, one long gun and three sets of night vision."

Cotton studied the young man for a moment.

"Why are you here?" Cotton asked.

"Just trying to... I don't know. Find my place I guess."

"Were you going to kill us?" Cotton asked. "If you had the chance?"

It was a calculated risk, Ralph knew it.

"Yes, sir, I reckon I would have. With the lights off."

"What do you mean?"

"It's easier to do things in the dark, things you wouldn't want brought to light. Maybe, I don't know, feels like God can't see what you're doing."

"You believe?" Cotton asked. "In God, I mean?"

"Reckon I do," Ralph replied.

"Care to meet Him?"

"Not quite yet, if it's all the same to you."

Cotton turned to Jean.

"What's your take?"

Holy smokes, Ralph thought to himself. *Is this girl going to decide if I live or die?*

Jean studied Ralph for a moment.

"Can't say it's a very Christian thing to kill other Christians," Jean said.

"Fair enough," Cotton agreed. He turned back to Ralph. "I'm going to tell you something, young man, because it may affect your behavior and determine if you live or die."

"Yes, sir," Ralph said.

"I was a member of Naval Special Warfare Development Group; you knew it as SEAL Team Six. I've killed more men than I care to count and some women, too. I'm not proud of the latter, but it happened. They showed up to a gunfight with a gun and I treated them like any adult who makes bad decisions. I can shoot faster, hit harder and ruck longer than any son of a bitch walking the earth at this point in time, I figure. I'm fixing to kill every man out there and stomp on their dead fucking skulls until I'm satisfied with the result of my efforts. Your only play is to stay put in that chair and not do anything stupid until it's all over."

"I can help you," Ralph said.

"No," Cotton said as he stood up. "You can't."

"I can!" Ralph protested urgently enough that it caught Cotton's attention. "There's more coming."

Cotton stopped. His grip tightened on his carbine.

"What do you mean 'more?'" Cotton asked.

"Randall Eisler's men. Harris sent a runner to Cypress Mill, and he's bound to come with more people." Ralph hesitated for a moment and then continued, "Maybe too many to take on. Even for you."

Cotton looked at Ralph for a moment and then back to Jean.

He signed something to her. This was the first time April had seen them do this. It must have meant they were saying something they didn't want anyone else to know.

What do you think? Cotton signed.

Feels like he's telling the truth, Jean signed back.

We don't need to be getting caught up in this, Cotton signed. *We move faster when we're on our own.*

Jean looked to April and then back to Cotton.

We told her we'd get her where she needs to go, Jean signed.

Cotton let out a sigh and then signed back.

I wish your memory wasn't so good.

So do I, Jean replied, but her face was serious. Cotton understood why. Things had happened, bad things that they couldn't take back. She didn't want to add one more to the list.

"Fine," Cotton said out loud. He turned back to Ralph. "How do you see this going down?"

"I ain't no Navy SEAL but I'm fast on a gun," Ralph said.

"Like you were in the hallway?" Cotton shot back.

"Man, are you kidding me? You're like death incarnate! I think I deserve a bit of slack for that one."

"Fair enough," Cotton agreed. "How's your long gun?"

"Better than it is bad," Ralph said. "I was never in the military, but I hunted with my daddy. I know scopes and I know how to hold for wind. I reckon I'm accurate out to five hundred yards with a sixteen-inch barrel and a good scope."

"Okay," Cotton said. "So, if I'm reading this situation right, you're saying you want to join up?"

"Yes, sir. If you'll have me."

"What if things don't go our way? Figure you'll join back up with the other side?"

Ralph was silent for a moment. Then he spoke.

"Funny thing about people. Maybe they don't know which way to go if they can't see the light, you know? Sun rises in the East and sets in the West and all that? You can't see the sun, how in the hell you gonna know which way to walk? Well, there hasn't been much sunlight in this world for a long time. Maybe that's why I threw in with the folks that I did. Maybe that's why I did things I wouldn't have done before all this. All I'm asking for now is a chance to redeem myself. That's all."

Cotton looked the young man over for a moment.

"I still don't trust you," Cotton said. He walked to the chair and cut Ralph loose. "You ain't gettin' a gun. You'll fight with your hands until I say otherwise."

Cotton pulled out a fresh zip tie and bound Ralph's left hand to the chair.

"How am I supposed to fight like this?" Ralph asked.

"For now, you're just a pair of eyes. Trouble comes, you call out."

Jean took up post beside the upstairs window that Cotton had established as their primary overwatch. Cotton had also set up Ralph in the downstairs kitchen, where he could surveil most of the eastern swath of land, but wouldn't be seen by the opposition force. He also figured if Ralph got squirrelly and tried to turn on them, he'd hear him coming.

The idea of bringing the young man into the fold still didn't sit right with him. However, even he had to recognize that if this Randall Eisler character showed up with more men, they would be seriously outgunned, potentially to an extent that even Cotton couldn't fight his way out of.

There was also something about Ralph's explanation and his behavior that seemed sincere.

April stood in the hallway with her AR at the ready. The woman looked as if she was getting some of her confidence back and shaking off the remnants of fear and adrenaline that had been flooding her system.

"How well you figure you can shoot that thing?" Cotton asked. "If it comes to it?"

"Up close, I can hit what I aim at," April said. "Out past twenty-five meters, I can't make any promises."

"That'll have to do," Cotton said. "I ain't been in many gun fights that went out past twenty-five meters, anyway. Hell, most were inside of ten."

"What do you think about this?" April asked. "He said more people are coming."

"I reckon they are," Cotton said with a nod. "Even if it's true, all we have to do is hold out until dark."

"Then you can take them?"

"Probably not," Cotton said. "Even with night vision, you hit a point where the fight's just too stacked against you. If I'm going up against twenty, thirty guys, even if they mostly can't see me coming, they'll eventually get lucky."

"So, what's the plan?"

"We'll sneak out," Cotton said. "Same way we moved last night."

"What about Ralph?" April asked.

Cotton could see that she was worried about the idea of taking the young man with them.

"Jury's still out on him," Cotton said. "As it stands right now, we don't take him. I need to see something from him before we go taking that kind of risk." He paused. "Just like I saw something out of you."

April nodded her understanding.

"Mind if I ask something?" April asked.

"More personal questions?" Cotton replied with a smile.

"Kind of. I just noticed you two speak sign language."

Cotton's face changed.

"You don't have to tell me why," April said quickly. "I should stop asking so many questions, maybe."

"No, it's fine," Cotton said. "Her grandmother, my mother, was deaf. Jean learned when she was young, mostly by watching me and her Gaga talk."

"Gaga?" April asked.

"Grandma. That was what she called her."

"Where is she now?" April stopped herself. "Shit. I'm sorry. That's not my business."

Cotton looked down at the floor.

"Same place everyone is," he said. "In one of the cities. Or not. Can't say that I know. Haven't seen or heard from her since this started."

"I'm sorry," April said.

"Nah," Cotton said. "We're curious. It's what makes us human. We have to hold on to as much of that as we can."

"You can ask me something, if you want," April said. "Even Steven, you know?"

"Sure," Cotton said. "Were you born out here? In Texas?"

"No. Actually, I was born in California."

"Holy shit," Cotton said. "That's it. Get out of this house."

April laughed.

"Daddy was in the army. I was born in San Luis Obispo outside of Camp Roberts. Not my fault. We got back to Texas once he finished his time."

"No one's perfect," Cotton said.

There was a pause for a moment.

"Is her ... mother still around?" April asked, sensing that she no longer needed to request permission to ask questions.

"She passed," Cotton said.

"Oh my God," April gasped. "I'm so sorry. Was it...?"

"No," Cotton replied. "It was a long time ago. She was a flight medic deployed to Afghanistan. Her helo went down, and she was missing for a while." Cotton's eyes drifted away for a moment and then came back. "They found her months later. She'd tried to run when they came down out of the mountains for her. Made it a long way. They eventually caught up with her."

There was silence. April looked back to the bedroom where Jean sat in a half kneeling position keeping watch.

"Maybe you should sleep," April said. "Just for a little while."

Cotton thought about it for a moment.

"Maybe you're right," he said. "I'll just close my eyes for a minute in that easy chair."

"I'll keep watch," April said. "I'll rouse you if anything happens."

Cotton looked at her for a moment and remembered what he had thought the other night. She was pretty in a hard, Texas kind of way. She looked back at him with her one milky white eye and one crystal blue.

"You should take the other one out," Cotton said, indicating the remaining contact. "We should all be who we are. Even if it isn't who we thought we wanted to be."

Kyle walked out into the tall grass beyond the oak tree that marked the group's perimeter. He knew it was breaking SOP (standard operating procedure) but he needed a damn break from the guys. Hearing that they might link up with Randall Eisler's group had been a bit of a relief, if he was being honest about it.

Sure, there was definitely something to be said for being their own men and not answering to anyone, but the same faces got old after a while. Not only that, but he'd heard there were women mixed in to Randall Eisler's group. That would be a hell of a thing. The only women they'd seen since they turned, well... that never ended very well.

Kyle stopped and realized that lost in his thoughts, he had not just wandered past the oak tree; he had gone way past it. He paid this no mind. After all, they were the most dangerous thing in this part of central Texas, aside from the odd rattlesnake.

Kyle unzipped his trousers and relieved himself

as he felt a cool breeze blow past him. That was quite nice after the way the sun had been baking them that day. He zipped up his trousers, and it was as he turned back to the tree that he heard the voice.

"Why do you think you were left behind?"

The voice was low and gravelly, but it sounded almost as if it resulted from an injury versus some tough guy act. It sounded diseased.

Kyle froze. He was face to face with a man who stood at least six foot four. He wore a tattered robe, his head was clean shaven and the sign of the cross was permanently carved into his forehead.

"No," Kyle said quietly.

Barnabas cocked his head to the side.

"That was not the question," Barnabas went on. "I asked you why you think you were left behind?"

The others came out of the field around Kyle. There were at least a dozen of them. They were the Nephilim.

Kyle knew the answer to the question. He'd heard the stories about this group.

"Because I'm a sinner," Kyle said quietly, attempting to steady his voice.

Kyle knew he should go for his gun. He'd left his AR back at the camp, but he still had his pistol on him. If he was fast enough; he could draw it.

Yet he didn't.

"We are here to prepare the earth for the return of Christ and the implementation of His plan," Barnabas said as he brought his hand from behind his back. He was holding a hammer. "Sinners are not part of His plan."

The others all brandished their own hammers.

Kyle stumbled back and his hand went for the pistol, but too late. A hammer struck his hand as it reached for the Glock 19, shattering every bone it made contact with. Barnabas drove his hammer forward horizontally, the same way he had so many times before.

The head of the hammer shattered Kyle's teeth and wedged inside of his jaw, breaking it and locking it at a sick angle. This silenced him as the rest of the men moved in, hammers striking in a macabre syncopated rhythm as they broke his bones and ground his body to a pulp.

Once his body had ceased its wild and frenzied jerks and his last breath of life escaped, the group turned their hammers to the claw end and went about the work they had engaged in for the past several months: prying the man apart, separating bone from muscle from tendon and organ.

Barnabas watched this calculated ballet of

horror unfold before him and he was pleased, because he knew that He would be pleased. The man turned to the tall grass and watched as Daniel 4 walked toward him. The man was a fierce warrior for the Nephilim, which was why his name had come from the 4th chapter of the book of Daniel.

Except that now, Daniel 4 looked troubled.

"What troubles you, brother?" Barnabas asked.

Daniel 4 looked to the destroyed body of Kyle and the group of Nephilim who were feeding upon him.

"Not troubled, brother. Rather... interested."

Barnabas smiled.

"Very well. What interests you?"

"There are more coming."

"Sinners?" Barnabas asked.

"Yes, brother. Perhaps many more."

"And this interests you?"

"This is the war we wanted," Daniel 4 said. "The war He wants."

Barnabas nodded. Occasionally, he became concerned that Daniel 4 was overly aggressive in his desire to be the warrior that God needed him to be, but still he respected the man's vigor.

"Agreed," Barnabas said. "If they are in such a

hurry to be sacrificed upon the altar of His greater glory, we will be more than happy to oblige them."

This seemed to please Daniel 4, and Barnabas touched him on the shoulder, indicating that he should leave him.

Barnabas turned and walked further out into the tall grass, to where he could see the farmhouse in the distance. He thought back to his dream the night before, and the vision that the Lord had brought to him.

The man in that house would kill him.

Randall Eisler stood outside of the "Processing House" as they called it. This was the place where they brought anyone the hunting parties tracked down, or who were unlucky enough to be found near the perimeter.

The work performed at the Processing House was simple. They decided who could be of use in a service role within the community and who would simply be food.

Randall Eisler admitted to himself that there were men who enjoyed this work a little too much for even his taste, but he understood they needed those men. It took a certain type of mentality to put a schoolteacher on his knees on a concrete floor and bash his head in with a sledgehammer.

Most folks didn't have that in them, and that was why so many had become food.

Randall Eisler's ability to recognize that 'talent' and put it to good use without letting it get out of control was a big part of what allowed them to survive. This was what had led to the formation of the "Slaughterhouse Five." While Randall Eisler highly doubted any of the five men in the group understood the reference, they seemed to take to the name all the same.

Randall Eisler stood in the doorway and he could feel the sun on his back, and that same sun turned the Processing House into an oven in the middle of the day. The caked blood and gore that slicked the floors sent an awful stench out that door.

This was by design. They were leading a hard life out there in the Texas Meat Belt, doing what they needed to do not only to survive, but to thrive. If folks were going to be passing out because of a little heat and some foul smells, best that they walked into the arms of their Creator sooner rather than later, and not waste his time.

The Slaughterhouse Five stood beside the doorway in their thick leather aprons, each man holding a different implement, any of which would have been fit for a horror movie. Meat hooks, an axe, a mallet and other such tools. The only thing missing was a chainsaw.

There were two dozen people scattered around the large room, some of whom had been there for a couple of weeks.

"Any prospects?" Randall Eisler asked.

The leader of the five was a man named Kevin, a former corrections officer who had spent most of his career at the Pollunsky Unit in Livingston, Texas. This particular prison in East Texas catered primarily to death row inmates and had a reputation for being one of the most brutal in the country. Within this brutal prison, Kevin McCarthy had carved himself out a niche as being as merciless as they came.

"Couple," Kevin said in his slow drawl. Every word he spoke sounded as if a great deal of thought was being put into it. He pointed to a man in the western corner of the room. This man was older, but seemed strangely calm. "That one over there. You ask me, seems like he thinks maybe he died a long time ago, and now he's just waitin' on Jesus to get around to comin' and collecting him."

Randall Eisler smiled at this. Kevin did have a

way with his hillbilly prose, even if he was borderline illiterate.

There was a knock at the door and Randall Eisler turned to see June Kennedy standing with her eyes locked on him. He knew that she didn't like to look into the Processing House. She had been in there once herself, waiting on her own death. When Randall Eisler asked her what she could do, she made a case that her secretarial skills could serve well in an organization such as his.

Randall Eisler thought it was a bunch of bullshit and she was just trying to save her own skin, but as things turned out, she was one hundred percent correct. Mrs. June Kennedy, formerly of Baton Rouge, Louisiana and the Effert and Sons Lumber Company, had been an instrumental cog in the finely tuned machine that she had transformed Cypress Mill into. It was even at the point where the men all called her ma'am, though she had made no such request. They addressed her by that title because they respected her.

"What is it, Miss Kennedy?" Randall Eisler asked. He wasn't about to address her as "ma'am" but he still gave due respect.

"It's about the men you sent up to Oatmeal,"

June said quietly. "They're heading to the house we sent that backup to for Harris and his men."

"Say what now?" Randall Eisler asked, practically spinning on his heels to face her.

June felt the shift in the room. The mood had changed, and she understood perfectly well why. None of this had been ordered.

"My understanding," June said slowly, calculating her words. "Is that the King is going as well, and asked them to accompany him. Jorge did call this in on the satellite phone."

Randall Eisler set his jaw. He didn't like this, not one bit. Perhaps most of all, he was irritated that Jorge has indeed followed protocol, and so he didn't really have anyone to be upset with. All the same, he could feel his ire elevating.

"I see," he said. Then he stopped and turned back to Kevin. "Wait a minute. Where's the sixth man?"

Kevin's eyes shifted to one of the other men.

"I wanted to expand the team," Randall Eisler said, stepping toward the Slaughterhouse Five. "I sent you that guy from Arkansas that came to the gate last week. Where is he now?"

Kevin let out a breath and locked eyes with his boss.

"He had an accident."

"Oh, really?" Randall Eisler asked. "Like the inmates at Pollunsky used to have 'accidents?'"

"Little bit," Kevin nodded. He paused for a moment and then continued. "We're the Slaughterhouse Five. Not the Slaughterhouse Six. With respect."

Shit, Randall Eisler thought to himself. *One thing you cannot do with folks you want to be mindless followers is give them a damn identity.*

"To be continued!" Randall Eisler snapped, pointing one of his long, nicotine-stained fingers at Kevin.

"They're asking for guidance," June went on. "Jorge is. And the young man. I imagine."

Randall Eisler nodded.

"Good," he said. "Good man. Tell him I'll meet him there."

"You'll meet him?" June asked incredulously.

"I am still allowed to leave the fucking compound!" Randall Eisler snapped, and immediately felt poorly for it. "Sorry, you didn't deserve that."

"I know," June said with a sly smile. "But I understand. How many men do you want?"

"All of them," Randall Eisler replied simply, standing a little taller. "Show of force."

June opened the small notebook she always kept in her left breast pocket.

"Sixty-seven," June said. "Sixty-seven fighters if you take all of them."

"Good."

"But," June went on. "You will leave the community undefended. Is that what you want?"

Randall felt his anger rising again, but pushed it back down. He knew that she was only trying to help.

"Fair enough," he said. "Set me up with an even forty."

June made a note in her book and then closed it and slid it back into her pocket.

"I assume departure in thirty is acceptable?" She asked.

"That will do nicely, thank you."

June turned and walked out the door and back into the old stockyard. Randall Eisler watched her walk away, and more specifically how the summer dress she wore slid across the curves of her body. She was ten years his senior, but that simple fact did nothing to change how she affected him.

Randall Eisler exited the Processing House and walked after her.

"Miss Kennedy?" Randall Eisler called.

June stopped and turned to face him.

"Yes, Randall Eisler?" She responded.

"Did you take it?"

She looked into his eyes.

"I did," she replied, and rolled up her sleeve to show a small band aid.

"Anything yet?" He asked.

"No," June replied. "But it's probably too soon to feel any effect."

"I wish you hadn't," Randall Eisler said. "Taken it, I mean."

"I know," June said. "I know that we both wanted there to be... more between us than there was, but now..."

"I know," Randall Eisler said. "If it works the way it's supposed to, you understand what you have to do."

"I've already packed my things," she said.

"You're going to have to run," Randall Eisler said. "Faster and farther than you ever have. I won't be able to hold them back. If they find you, it'll be— it'll be—"

June held up a hand to silence him.

"You don't have to say it," June said. "I knew the consequences when I asked for this."

"Is it that bad?" Randall Eisler asked. "Who we are?"

"It's not what I want," June replied. "When I thought there was no way out, I leaned into it as best I could."

"But it's not who you are."

"Maybe it's not who any of us are," June said. "Maybe it's just what we made ourselves believe we could be so we could sleep through the night."

"Shit."

Harris stood in the area past the big oak tree Denny had brought him and Bob to. He looked down at the dismembered body of what used to be Kyle Parker. It was very clear what had happened, and more specifically, who had done it.

"That's the understatement of the century," Bob said.

Denny stood silently; the color drained from his face. It wasn't that he had never seen this before. Hell, they had done it to plenty of people, but somehow the way they did it was human. They never pulled people apart while they were still alive.

It was always clean. A single round in the back of the head and then strip the carcass, just like you'd do for a deer. Not like this.

There was also the issue of cannibals eating other cannibals. They all knew it happened, but there was a sort of unwritten law about not doing this kind of thing. As long as there were 'normals' walking the earth, they went down first. You didn't eat your own kind. It just wasn't... civilized.

"No sign?" Harris asked and turned to Denny. "No sign of who did this?"

"No, sir," Denny said quietly.

Bob looked around the field and then back to Harris.

"This wasn't just a couple of guys," Bob said. "This was at least—"

"Let me guess," Harris said with a smirk. "Ten?"

"Don't mock me!" Bob shouted. This caught Harris' attention. The much bigger man was clearly angry. Maybe even afraid.

"I apologize," Harris said and held up a hand in a placating gesture.

Bob relaxed his posture.

"You know more than you're saying," Harris said. He had always suspected as much, but had never pushed.

For a moment, Bob's eyes were far away, almost disjointed, and then they snapped into focus and settled on Harris.

"It's a long story," Bob said.

"You know," Harris said. "One upside to the world ending is we've got nothing but time. So, if you're willing to tell what you know, I think I need to hear it."

"I was one of them. In the beginning, in the very beginning. You know I only joined up with you a few months ago, but we didn't talk about where I was before that. I kept it to myself and you respected that decision. I didn't talk about it because odds are pretty good you would have sent me packing. At best.

"In the beginning, the group was small. It was actually my old church. The congregation was holding it together pretty well, what with everything happening. We kept services going, did community outreach, the whole nine yards. We thought we could make it through. I suppose a lot of us, in the back of our heads, we knew it was the end times but we just couldn't deal with it. Couldn't accept that it had finally come. No one thought they were ready for that.

"Then when the vaccine came around, we did the same thing everyone else did. We took it. Then we turned. Even during that, though, we stayed strong. We kept up services, kept up our outreach. It was hard. We started losing folks. Some to suicide, some headed for the FEMA camps and others just went to the wilderness.

"It was just the day after the President was shot that he came around. This man. He was a preacher from Little Rock, or at least that's what he said. Called himself Barnabas. He was one of those sorts, those men who can just pull people in with his words. He was a big boy, too. My height, around six foot four, but just freaking big. Like maybe he used to be a bodybuilder or something.

"He just walked into the church one day and took the pulpit. Damndest thing I've ever seen. Pastor Steve tried to get him to leave at first, but then Barnabas leaned in and said something to him real quiet like. Still don't know what it was he said, but Pastor Steve nodded his head and sat down in one of the front pews.

"We had taken the mark of the beast. That's what Barnabas said. First damn words out of his mouth. We had taken the vaccine and therefore we had taken the mark. He laid it all out, and it made sense. The mark had made beasts of man. That's what we were: beasts. It all made sense. The important part was that there was a way out of it, a way out of damnation, a way to still be of service to the Lord. We would become the Nephilim.

"You remember them? The fallen angels from Genesis? We were the fallen angels now, the men who became beasts, but we could redeem ourselves by cleansing the unclean from the earth before Jesus returned.

"Saying it out loud now, it all sounds so crazy, but back then, it was all we had. We were also just hungry all the time. Originally we were Gatherers, just getting by on what we could find.

"The Nephilim, according to the Bible, were all giants, which is how we ended up with our selection process. There is no Nephilim out there walking with Barnabas who is under six feet tall. Not only that, but they're all strong. Freakishly strong. That's what happens if a cannibal gorges himself on human flesh. Very few do that. We actually eat pretty light compared to what we're capable of.

"We would hunt people down. Ones, twos, or even entire groups. Anyone over six feet tall had a choice to join or die. Some of them faked their allegiance to keep drawing breath, and we knew that, but it didn't take long having Barnabas in your ear every hour of every day to become a believer. There were a couple that never bought into it, but they didn't fool Barnabas. He would eventually dispose of them.

"Thing about Barnabas is that it's not a scam. The man isn't a con artist or some crazy cult leader. He believes to his core in everything he is saying and everything he is doing. He truly believes that the righteous were taken from the Earth during the rapture, and that he has been called upon to cleanse the earth of the beasts and the unclean before the return of Christ.

"When someone has that level of belief, it's contagious. Maybe just like the virus was."

Harris was in disbelief after hearing Bob recount his origin story. Denny was even more shaken than before.

"What you're saying," Harris said, "is that there is an army of literal giant cannibals stalking central Texas who think we have to be wiped out to make room for Jesus because we're the unclean?"

"Well, if you want to get technical about it, we're the beasts. The unvaccinated are the unclean," Bob corrected him. "And I did tell you. About most of it."

"You just left out the part about you being one of 'em."

"You know damn well if I told you all that, you would have sent me on my way."

"Damn right," Harris said.

"And to be truthful about it, I just never thought we'd run into them again. Central Texas is a big place."

"Wait a minute," Harris said. "You left out one part. Why did you leave? Why ain't you still huntin' cannibal beasts and unclean anti-vaxxers?"

"Toward the end, it started getting darker. Barnabas said we had to anoint ourselves in the eyes of the Lord. That was when he started carving crosses into everyone's foreheads. Something about that, I don't know. It just flipped a switch in my brain. I ran."

"How many were you?" Harris asked. "Back then?"

"That was six months ago," Bob said. "We were forty strong at that point."

"How much you figure he built up in the six months since then?"

"We were only twelve in the beginning, and his

growth was exponential." Bob thought about it for a moment. "There might be a hundred of them by now."

"A hundred?" Harris nearly shouted, and his eyes grew wide. "I thought we were dealing with maybe a score of disorganized half-starved lunatics out there! At best!"

"Why do you think I wanted to leave?" Bob asked.

Harris turned to Denny as if he suddenly remembered that the young man was still standing there.

"This stays with us, you understand?" Harris said. "We can't have the boys panicking."

"I understand," Denny said quickly, and Harris could indeed see that the young man understood. Something about Bob's story had not only not eaten away at his resolve, it seemed to have bolstered it.

"Harris!" A voice called out from the perimeter.

It was Vince Welch, one of the older men in the group, running toward them.

"What now?" Harris griped.

Vince slowed down as he approached the three men. He looked down at Kyle's remains.

"Holy shit! What in the hell happened to him?"

"We'll get to it," Harris said and raised his hand to calm the man down. "What's going on?"

Vince's eyes lingered on the body for a moment longer and then found his leader.

"Just got word back from our runner. Randall Eisler is sending forty men."

"Well, at least there's some good news," Harris said.

"And he's coming with them," Vince followed up.

"Shit!" Harris snapped. "Well, that is not what I wanted to hear." There was something in Vince's eyes that told him there was more to the story. "What else is there?"

"The King is coming too."

"What?" Bob spat. "How in the hell did he get involved?"

"Can't quite say as I know," Vince said. "Either way, he's coming soon with his own men."

"How many?" Harris asked.

"Don't know," Vince replied.

"Hm," Harris said and rocked back on his heels. "This could work for us."

"This could be a slaughter," Bob shot back.

Harris put a hand on Bob's shoulder and led him away and out of earshot. He turned to the taller man.

"Denny will keep his mouth shut," Harris said slowly. "I know he will."

"What are you suggesting?" Bob asked.

"We could take it all," Harris said. "In one fell swoop. This character, Barnabas, and these Nephilim of his. They're really serious. Guy in that house, just in case you forgot about him, he's serious too. We're about to have a damn army descend on this place between Randall Eisler's men and whoever the King is bringing."

Bob understood.

"Just let it happen?"

Harris shrugged.

"Once folks start firing shots, we go to ground. Just take a step back and let them sort each other out. Then we make a beeline to Cypress Mill and take it by force. If Randall Eisler's coming with that many men, won't be much left to defend it."

"And then to Oatmeal," Bob surmised.

"It's not the craziest idea I've ever had."

"No," Bob said. "It is, but that doesn't mean it won't work."

CHAPTER 8

"They're going to notice we're gone," Sylvester said as Dane worked the lock on the door with his lock pick kit. "I'm telling you, any minute now."

"Shut it," Matt said sharply as he performed a brass check on his AR and indexed his pistol. "By the time they notice we're gone, this'll all be over."

"What makes you think we're going to fare any better against this guy than everyone else did?" Dane asked.

"Because the first group didn't know what they were getting into and Ralph and Milton were a couple of dumbasses."

"Milton fought in the damn UFC!" Dane shot back.

"Yeah, and he lost every match," Sylvester said as he felt the lock click open.

Reaching out, Sylvester slowly opened the door and pushed it ajar just enough to let some light in.

Matt grabbed Dane by the shoulder and spun him around.

"Get your head in the game!" Matt snapped. "We're about to be damn heroes, but not if you keep whining like this. You understand?"

"Yeah," Dane replied and brought his carbine up.

There was nothing more to be said. They were going to do this.

Sylvester pushed the door the rest of the way open and entered the living room quickly but quietly. The other two came in behind them. They had done this before. When the world was still somewhat sane, the men had taken Close Quarters Battle classes out in Houston with a group of former Special Forces guys that trained civilians.

When they came back home, they'd found some abandoned houses outside of Leander where they practiced. For what, they did not know. It was just a way to kill time and fantasize about a world where they had chosen a different path than working as welders.

Then it wasn't a fantasy anymore, and they were doing it for real. They weren't half bad at it either. They eventually threw in with Harris and his boys and had done several hits since then, when it was warranted. Considering this, Matt was all the more surprised and disappointed when they weren't the first ones the boss sent in.

So, they took matters into their own hands.

Matt entered the house last and picked up his corner, with a short hallway that led into the kitchen. That was when he saw him. It was that kid Ralph. He was sitting in the kitchen, flex-cuffed to a chair with half his face smashed in.

Matt locked eyes with Ralph and put his finger to his lips, indicating that the man had better not give them away. Ralph looked unsure, so Matt drove his point home by directing the muzzle of his rifle toward him.

Ralph nodded his understanding.

Matt turned back to the rest of his team and the three men flowed out of the living room and into the hallway that fed into the main stairwell.

It was quiet. Sylvester was at the front of the pack and he stopped at the foot of the stairs. He nodded to the floor. Matt and Dane had been so caught up in their forward movement to the stairwell that they almost missed Milton's body on the floor.

This sent a shock of fear down Dane's spine.

Milton's body was completely butchered.

Jesus Christ! That's Milton! Whoever this guy is, he sure did a number on him, Dane thought to himself, but then pushed it aside. If he didn't want some of the same, he knew he better get on task. Then a macabre thought entered his mind. *We set this house up to be a trap, but what if we're now the ones in it?*

Sylvester stepped onto the stairs and was quiet. He held for a moment and then continued moving up the stairway. The other two followed behind him. They stayed focused on the first doorway at the second-floor landing. That was where the man in the house had to be. He sure as hell wasn't on the first floor. He had to be in that room.

Sylvester hit the second-floor landing and closed in toward the door. He now had his weapon up and watched the Holosun red dot as he inched closer to that door. He turned forty-five degrees, and that was when he saw him.

The guy looked like a retired biker. He was asleep.

Holy shit! Sylvester thought to himself. *Did we actually catch this son-of-a-bitch during his nap?*

Cotton opened his eyes. He smiled.

"No!" Dane felt the words spilling out of his mouth, almost as if he were vomiting them up out of fear. His legs went weak. This was like something out of a horror novel.

Jean Wiley stepped from around the corner to their right, put her Hellcat pistol flush with Sylvester's temple and pulled the trigger.

Dane watched Sylvester's head explode with blood in front of him, some of it splattering across the girl's face. She was just a girl.

Sylvester's legs dropped out from beneath him like a rag doll and he collapsed.

April stepped away from the wall to their left where she had been holding position inside the room, raised the AR to her shoulder and fired through the wall, from inside the room to outside on the landing. The 5.56 rounds made quick work of the weak drywall and tore through both Dane and Matt.

Dane felt his body crash back against the railing. He knew he'd been hit, but did not know how many times. The railing cracked as his spine struck it and his weapon fell from his hands as he crashed to the floor. With great pain, he turned his head and saw Matt lying halfway down the stairs. The man's neck was at an odd angle, and his eyes were locked open. He was dead.

The girl stood over Dane. Blood splattered her face, and she stared at him through cold blue eyes. Cotton walked up behind her.

"I can do it," he said, and put his hand on her shoulder.

Jean looked into Dane's eyes.

"No," she said. "I can do it."

"As long as you remember," Cotton said. "That sometimes you gotta show mercy. Even out here. Maybe not now, but sometimes."

Jean raised the Hellcat and pointed it at the spot between Dane's eyes. The killbox. Her finger picked up the slack on the trigger.

"Mercy don't make the grass grow."

Cotton moved quickly down the stairs and found Ralph in the kitchen, his left arm still flex cuffed to the chair.

Ralph looked up at him expectantly.

"You did good," Cotton said with a nod.

"They weren't half bad at hitting houses," Ralph

said. "But they were always shit at sneaking up on them."

This was true. Ralph had seen them coming from far away and alerted Cotton, who then set the plan in motion. The idea behind the ruse had been that while Ralph saw people coming, he couldn't be one hundred percent certain how many they were. It could have been three, but it also could have been ten.

Jean and April had set up in hiding to take out the first element of the assault force, after which Cotton would attack directly and do his best to finish the rest. Fortunately, it hadn't ended up that way, and there had been no follow up attack.

"Well, you bought yourself some good will."

"Enough to get rid of this?" Ralph asked, indicating the flex cuff.

"Not quite yet," Cotton replied and walked away.

Ralph didn't bother protesting. Despite knowing very little about Cotton Wiley, he understood that once the man had his mind set on something, not a thing in heaven or hell was likely to move him an inch in either direction.

Once satisfied that there was not some other assault element about to make entry, Cotton ascended the steps again and turned to the left to see April and Jean in the second-floor bathroom. As he suspected when they first arrived at the house, there was indeed running water.

April dabbed at Jean's face with a half clean rag, scrubbing the blood from her flesh as the girl stared at herself in the mirror. Jean's eyes were blank. Cotton saw this, he saw it and it worried him. He walked to the bathroom and looked at his daughter's reflection in the mirror.

"Are you okay?" He asked.

"Yeah," she replied. "Not my first time."

"I know," Cotton said.

The truth of it was that it wasn't even her first time killing a man up close like that. He thought back to the car in Arkansas when she had shot that man while he was on top of her.

Jean stared at her father in the mirror and she could tell he was lost in thought.

"I'm fine," she insisted. "I did what had to be done."

"Right," Cotton said. He pulled the Hellcat out of his cargo pocket and held it out to her. He had taken it from her hand after she shot the man in the hallway. "Here."

Jean looked at it for a moment, like she didn't know what it was. She looked up at her father.

"I saw one of those boys in the hall had a Glock 19 on him. I want that."

"Why?" Cotton asked. "Seems like this has served you pretty well."

"Only takes eleven rounds," Jean said. "Glock 19 takes fifteen plus one and the bigger mags. Besides, you said the Hellcat was for old ladies and men with small hands, of which I ain't either."

Cotton laughed. He had said that. He still hadn't learned to watch what he said around kids.

Without another word, he turned and walked across the second-floor landing, then down the stairs where he had lain the bodies of the dead men. He had no plans to drag them all outside, as they shouldn't be there long enough for decomposition to become an issue.

True enough, one man had a nice Glock 19 with some decent stipling on the grip. The improved texture that the stipling provided would help her recoil control as she became accustomed to the larger weapon. It wasn't as big as Cotton's Glock 17 (about an inch shorter on the barrel and the grip) but still bigger than the Hellcat.

He pulled the gun from the holster and then took

the time to unhook the holster from the man's belt as well. He'd come back later to strip the rest of the mags and ammo from the bodies.

Cotton walked back up the stairs and found April and Jean waiting in the bedroom. He held out the pistol. Jean took it and couldn't suppress a smile. She checked that the weapon had a round in the chamber and then also took the holster and looped her belt through it, then secured everything in place.

Cotton felt a shift in his perception of her. If he was keeping track of time correctly, her thirteenth birthday would be in about a month. He looked at her with the gun on her hip and her jaw set. Her face was resolute. Just like her mother's. She was her mother's daughter. Not only that, but she was no longer a little girl. Somewhere in the recent past, she had become a woman.

"What makes the grass grow, Fancy Face?" Cotton asked.

"Blood, Senior Chief," Jean replied. "Blood makes the grass grow."

"You two are creepy," April said, only half-joking.

She and Cotton sat on the hallway floor with

their backs to the railing, watching Jean sleep in the easy chair.

Cotton smiled. He pulled a cigarette out of his pocket and lit it, then inhaled deeply. He hadn't had one in quite a while. Partially because light and smoke were a pretty easy way to give away your position and draw the wrong kind of attention, and because cigarettes weren't exactly easy to come by. Even the cannibals still smoked and had sucked up most of the supply.

"Don't you know you aren't supposed to smoke inside?" April asked.

"Don't you know you aren't supposed to eat people?" Cotton quipped.

April's face fell.

"Shit," Cotton said. "I'm sorry. Bad joke."

"No kidding," April said quietly and then changed the subject. "What was that about? After you gave her the gun?"

"The grass thing?" Cotton asked, understanding what she was referencing.

"Yeah."

"Something we used to say in the Teams," he replied. "What makes the grass grow? Blood, Senior Chief."

"You must be a riot at parties," April said.

"It's just the culture," Cotton explained. "Call it gallows humor or brainwashing or whatever you want. We have to see the world differently to do the things we're tasked with. Anyway, I used to answer the door like that at the house. Team guy would knock and that was my challenge. What makes the grass grow?"

"Blood, Senior Chief," April replied.

"That's right. She must have heard that, I don't know. A thousand times? Now we use it as a security challenge if we ever need to. If we're separated and she hears someone coming but isn't sure it's me, she'll call out 'What makes the grass grow?' If she doesn't hear the right answer, she runs."

"I don't think that girl has got much running left in her," April said. "Seems more like a fighter."

April studied Cotton for a moment.

Then she leaned in.

Then she kissed him.

He kissed her back.

April pressed her hands into his chest and pushed him away, recoiling from his touch.

"What is it?" Cotton asked, confused by her reaction.

"You smell good," April said. "Too good."

Cotton understood. He smelled like dinner.

"Don't forget what I am," April said. "Just in case I do."

Barnabas walked up the small hill where Daniel 4 was standing with Job 3 and Ezekiel 9.

"Two sets of vehicles," Daniel 4 said and pointed to a road in the distance. "Coming from different directions."

"Interesting," Barnabas said. "How many men?"

"In total? Perhaps forty. Maybe more."

"Not enough," Job 3 said.

Barnabas smiled at that.

"True, brother. Not nearly enough. Still, we must prepare properly. We must not grow overconfident." He turned to Ezekiel 9. "Are the supplies still in the tunnels?"

"Yes," Ezekiel 9 said with a nod.

"Take me to them."

Barnabas, Ezekiel 9 and Daniel 4 walked back down the hill, leaving Job 3 to his watch. They walked through a field of drying grass until they arrived at a large mound with an entrance to an old mine partially obscured by wire fencing.

From within this ancient mine shaft emerged

three Nephilim, covered in dirt and carrying pick-axes and shovels.

"How goes your work?" Barnabas asked the three.

"Quite well," one said, and the other two nodded their agreement.

Barnabas walked past them and into the tunnel with Daniel 4 and Ezekiel 9. The three men entered a large chamber within the mine where supplies were stacked, and beyond that, two other tunnels split off into the darkness.

"It is quite a marvel," Barnabas said. "How much work has been done here in His name."

"Agreed, brother," Daniel 4 said. "We believe that these tunnels now stretch for miles beneath the surface."

Daniel 4 opened a crate and pulled from it a military plate carrier, complete with two SAPI plates.

"Won't the Lord protect us?" Ezekiel 9 asked, the tone of his voice unsure. "What need have we for these?"

Barnabas smiled.

"This is how He protects us, brother. Never ignore the obvious gifts that the Lord has sent you in favor of a search for mysticism."

Ezekiel 9 nodded his understanding.

"I have a task for you," Barnabas went on. He reached into another crate and removed a KA-Bar knife. He handed it to Ezekiel 9. "This needs to be quiet. Quieter than can be done even with a hammer."

Ezekiel took the knife. He looked at it and then to Barnabas.

"What will you have me do? What is it you ask of me?"

"I ask nothing of you," Barnabas said. "He asks of you all that you have."

"Of course," Ezekial 9 said.

"We need to send a message. To the man in that house."

"What will the message be?" Ezekiel 9 asked.

Barnabas looked at him coldly.

"You are not as safe as you think you are."

"What in the hell did those idiots think they were doing?" Harris shouted as he stood before the group of men he had positioned at the bottom of the ravine.

One man spoke up.

"I saw them leaving," Damien said. "I should

have stopped them. I didn't know what they were going to do."

Harris wanted to berate the man, but he knew he was telling the truth. It looked like Sylvester, Matt and Dane had gone off on their own to take the house. He knew they thought they were a bunch of CQB experts, and they were pretty damn good, but apparently not that good.

Twenty minutes earlier, both Bob and Harris had heard the bursts of gunfire erupt from the house. This caused some confusion, as neither of them had ordered an assault or even a reconnaissance of the area. They had observation posts set at three points around the structure, but they were all at least one hundred yards out, and there was no reason any of them should engage the occupants.

This had all led to the realization that three men had taken it upon themselves to end the standoff that had been going on all day.

Harris waited a moment longer and then let out a breath.

"We have to hold fast," he said. "Re-enforcements are on the way. Once they get here, we're going to bulldoze this guy and then it'll be a new day."

"New day?" One man asked.

Harris surveyed the group for a moment. He wasn't sure how they were going to take the news.

"Look, the landscape has changed. Things aren't the way they were a year ago. Hell, even a month ago. World's changing and it's changing fast. We need to change with it." He paused again, mostly for effect. "You've all heard about the second vaccine by now. You also know that they say it can undo what the first one did. Word has it they're about to administer it in the cities and they're even sending it out into the country, no questions asked. The King's got it. Even Randall Eisler's got it. We can get it too, but we're going to have to move into the fold."

Some men smiled at this, while others clearly had a different opinion.

"Treaty members?" Damien asked. "You're saying we'd become treaty members?"

"That's about the size of it," Bob chimed in.

"I thought we were our own men," Damien protested.

"We still are," Harris said. "But we've gotta be realistic about it. We're not just throwing in with Randall Eisler, no questions asked. We'll have our demands and those demands will need to be met."

"And there's another reason," Bob said and

looked at Harris. He knew the man didn't want to talk about the Nephilim.

"Well," Harris said. "Yes. There's something else. We're not alone out here."

"The ones that killed Kyle!" Vince Welch called out. "The ones with the crosses."

"That's right," Harris confirmed. "There's another group out here. Other cannibals. They're well organized and they're dangerous. They call themselves the Nephilim."

"How many?" Damien asked.

Harris looked to Bob and then back to Damien.

"We don't know," Harris said. "Could be fifty, could be a hundred."

"A hundred?" Damien asked in disbelief.

"See, that's why we need the backup," Harris went on. "In the beginning, all these groups were small, just like we were. Now they're getting bigger."

"Groups are becoming armies," Bob said.

"And armies go to war," Harris concluded. "So, it's not just about rooting this son-of-a-bitch out of that house. Now it's about survival."

A radio on Vince's belt went off and he stepped back from the group and keyed the push-to-talk. He listened for a moment and then turned back to Harris.

"Vehicles coming from two different directions," Vince relayed.

"Two directions?" Harris asked.

"North and West, I'd guess," Bob surmised. "Coming from Oatmeal and Cypress Mill."

"The King is coming?" Vince asked.

"Look," Harris said. "I just need you to trust me. This is all gonna work out. Either way, can't undo it now."

"What if we don't want it?" Damien asked. "The vaccine. What if we want to stay the way we are?"

"I second that," another man said.

"Let's cross that bridge when we come to it," Harris said. "For now, we need to focus on survival."

Cotton stood in the window and watched the sun dropping in the sky. He checked his watch. It wouldn't be long before the sun disappeared. That would be their time to get the hell out of this place.

He was standing a few feet from the actual window, far enough that he wouldn't be an easy target for some sniper set up in the tall grass or further down the road. He thought about that for a moment. Should they just follow that same road they took in to get out and back to the interstate? Might as well. Under cover of night and under NODs, they should have a pretty clear go of it.

As he stared at the long country road, he saw dust. Then he saw a reflection. Then he saw the first truck.

"What in the hell?" He muttered.

April walked up behind him.

"Vehicles?" She asked.

Cotton walked to his rucksack and retrieved his binoculars. He returned to the window and focused them on the distance he wanted to see clearly. Sure enough, he was looking at vehicles. Not just one, or two or even three, but seven trucks and SUVs coming from the West. All were packed full of fighters.

"Shit," he said quietly and handed the binos to April.

She scanned the road as well and then lowered them. She looked at Cotton.

"I know those trucks," she said.

"Cypress Mill?" He asked.

"Randall Eisler's men. Whoever this guy is, he must have called them in like Ralph said. They must be Treaty Members."

Cotton took the binos back and scanned the horizon. His eyes stopped on the main road coming from the north.

"This just keeps getting better," he said as he watched three more trucks coming from a different direction.

"More?" April asked, the rising panic in her voice clear.

Cotton lowered the binos and turned to her.

"It's fine," he said firmly. "Believe it or not, I've been in worse spots than this. You just have to believe we're going to make it. If you lose that, there's no coming back from it."

"We're going to get out of this," April said firmly.

"Damn right," Cotton said. "Now I need you to get downstairs and cut Ralph loose."

"What?" April asked in disbelief.

"It's Hail Mary time," Cotton said. "We need every gun we can get. He could have screwed us when those three idiots tried to bum rush the house, but he didn't. It's a risk, but it's a risk we have to take."

"Okay," April said. She still did not seem quite convinced, but she trusted Cotton.

Cotton watched her leave the room and then walked to where Jean was asleep in the easy chair.

"We're going to get out of this," he said to himself.

They had to.

He nudged his daughter awake and her eyes fluttered for a moment before her grip tightened on the MK18 carbine and she sat up.

"What's happening?" She asked.

"Inbound," Cotton replied. "A lot of inbound."

"Okay," Jean replied. She stood up and tightened the sling on her rifle, then indexed the pistol on her belt. She looked out the window and could see the dust further down the road from the line of vehicles. "What's the plan?"

"Still working on that part," he replied as he secured his helmet complete with mounted night vision.

Jean knew what this meant. He thought there was a possibility they would fight into the night and that it would be intense enough that he wouldn't even have time to mount the RNVGs. She watched her father's eyes dart around the room and saw that he was breathing through his mouth.

She reached out and put her hand on his arm. Cotton stopped what he was doing and looked at her.

"Hey," Jean said. "We're going to be fine."

"I know," Cotton said.

"No," Jean said. "What I mean is that we might die here in this house. Tonight. But if we do, we'll get to see Mom again. No matter what happens, we're going to come out on top."

Cotton wasn't sure what to say, and before he thought of something, they were interrupted by April shouting from downstairs.

"Get down here!" She screamed. "Now!"

Cotton was out of the room like a shot. It was all reflex, all training. He bolted down the stairs at the low ready, saw no one in the living room, cleared the hall to the back door and then snaked around the room toward the kitchen. He knew that Jean was right behind him.

Then he stopped. He lowered his rifle.

"Jesus," he said.

Ralph was still flex cuffed to the chair, but his throat had been cut open and someone had stabbed him over a dozen times in the chest. There was a piece of tape over his mouth.

Cotton looked at April.

"I didn't do this!" She shouted. "I found him like this!"

Cotton brought his weapon back up and moved through the rest of the house, checking every room, every closet, and under every bed. Nothing. They were alone.

"How in the hell did this happen?" He asked.

"Could someone have been in here with us the whole time?" Jean asked. "Then done this and left?"

"Or come and gone?" April asked.

"No," Cotton said firmly. "There's no way. One of us would have heard something. Ralph would have said something!"

Outside, they could hear the vehicles getting closer.

"We don't have time for this," Cotton said. He looked at his watch again. They had less than an hour until sunset.

"Ralph said they have night vision," April said. She knew Cotton was waiting for the sun to set.

"Having night vision is like having a gun. If you don't know how to use it, it doesn't mean shit."

April said nothing. She had no choice but to have faith in Cotton Wiley. She looked at Jean and could see that the young girl was holding fast. At that moment, she decided she would too. She had no other choice.

.   .   .

Randall Eisler leaned forward in the passenger seat of the old Bronco and looked at the house in the distance. Then his eyes moved back to the group of men they were rolling up to. They were all outfitted well enough, but seemed disorganized to him, all walking around with seemingly no structure.

Then he saw a familiar face. Harris Hawthorne. He'd met the former insurance salesmen once before, months prior, when Harris did him the courtesy of notifying him he was operating in the area. Harris had refused Randall Eisler's offer of protection and potentially joining the treaty. A lesser man might have been upset by this, but Randall Eisler understood.

However, understanding, like most things, had a limit, and that limit had come. In the beginning, it was just a handful of cockroaches running around what had become the Texas Meat Belt. Harris had boasted a dozen men. By the look of it, he now had nearly thirty.

"That son-of-a-bitch sure grew his organization," Randall Eisler said wonderingly.

"Probably by accident," his driver, Mitchell, said from behind the wheel.

"Probably," Randall Eisler agreed. "Either way, we can use that manpower. If he folds in with us, we'll be bumping up against the same number of soldiers the King has."

Mitchell said nothing. If there was more to that statement, he didn't want to know about it. He pulled the Bronco to a stop away from the group and cut the engine. The rest of the vehicles stopped behind him, but everyone stayed put. They all knew the protocol. No reason to pile out of vehicles with weapons and spook the locals.

Randall Eisler stepped out of the truck and walked in front of it.

Harris Hawthorne broke from the cluster of men that had been surrounding him with Bob in tow.

The two men stopped and faced each other.

Randall Eisler looked to the house and then back to Harris.

"He in there?" Randall Eisler asked.

"Figure he still is," Harris said.

"Important for you to get him out, is it?"

"Important enough to throw in with you."

Randall Eisler smiled and extended his hand. Harris shook it and returned the smile, though something in his eyes told Randall Eisler it wasn't one hundred percent genuine.

"I get it," Randall Eisler said. "We can't have people running around central Texas thinking they can do whatever the hell they want. Specially if they're dealing with Treaty Members."

Harris took a step forward and lowered his voice.

"There are conditions," he said. "You understand. Things that need to be sorted out. The men have concerns."

"I understand that," Randall Eisler said with a nod. "Think of this as a show of goodwill. We're gonna help you sort this problem out and then we can go from there."

Bob raised his hand.

"Yes..." Randall Eisler said and paused, clearly wanting the man's name.

"Bob," he offered.

"Yes, Bob."

Bob looked at Harris and then back to Randall Eisler.

"Some men have concerns about the new vaccine," Bob said.

Randall Eisler smiled. He had been expecting this question would come up, just perhaps not so soon.

"Ah, yes. We do have the vaccine."

"Has anyone taken it yet?" Harris asked.

Randall Eisler looked at his watch.

"Should be taking the second batch right about now," he said. "Your men on board with that?"

"Some," Harris said. "Not sure how many. Don't think we'll really know until it's real."

"Agreed," Randall Eisler said. "We're in the same boat. Lot of folks said they wanted it and then decided they didn't. Others swore they wouldn't take it and they're getting it right now." He paused for a moment, seeming to think about it further. "But we had to have a ruling concerning the vaccine. You know, cannibals and normals, they can't live together. Don't make a lick of sense to try."

"Ex-communication," Bob surmised.

"More like a running start," Randall Eisler said with a smile. "And the folks taking the vaccine understand that when and if they turn back, they'll have twenty-four hours to get the hell out of dodge. After that point, best believe we'll be looking for them. Same thing would apply to your men."

"You're not taking it?" Harris asked.

"You know, I was in the Texas National Guard back in the day: 36th Infantry Division. Ended up doing two deployments to Iraq before my time was up. On that first deployment, I killed a man day one in country. First damn day. There were others, but that first one, I tell you... it changed me. I went from being just like any other guy out there to being a killer. That kind of change, you can't take it back. Can't ever take it back. Even if you get a regular Joe job, start a family and never fire a gun again, you'll always be that killer. I think this is the same thing. Even if that vaccine does turn folks back from canni-bals to humans, you're still that same meat eater," Randall Eisler said and pointed to his chest. "In here. So, I think walking around with them human eyes, maybe living in some place with other folks but always knowing you ate people just like you, you'll go crazy."

There was silence for a moment.

"So, that's a no," Bob said.

"Hell no, I ain't taking no vaccine!" Randall Eisler shouted.

From behind them came the sound of another engine, and the three men turned and saw three more vehicles coming their way, albeit more up to date and clearly better maintained than the ones Randall Eisler had shown up in.

"Well," Randall Eisler said. "This circus just gained a few more monkeys."

CHAPTER 9

COTTON WALKED BACK up the stairs and stopped at the second-floor landing. He'd done an intensive search of the entire house that turned up nothing. If there was still someone in there with him, he was a damn magician.

He could see April and Jean in the bedroom, both sitting with their ARs at the ready. They were depending on him. The only problem was, he had no idea how in the hell they were going to get out of this.

"Any new developments?" He asked as he walked into the room.

"No more vehicles coming," April said. "At least that's something. They're all parked in the ravine."

Cotton thought back to something he had seen in

the kitchen pantry: cans of lighter fluid. He tapped one of his long fingers on the stock of his rifle and let out a breath.

"I think I have a plan," Cotton said slowly.

April looked at him and could see something in his eyes.

"It's not a good one, is it?" She asked.

"No," Cotton replied. "It's not."

"Bad plan now is better than a perfect one too late," Jean said. "What is it?"

"Set the house on fire," Cotton said.

"This is good," April replied. "We'll get all the truly insane ideas out of the way before we get to the just plain bad ones."

"No, think about," Cotton went on. "We need a distraction. That tall grass behind the house is only ten meters away. We Just have to make it that far and we can disappear. They're most likely to come at us either from the front or from that ravine. Even if they do surround the place, we can get through that one cluster."

Everyone was silent for a moment, then Jean spoke up.

"This can work," she said. "We've got water in this house. We can cover ourselves with wet blankets to protect from the heat. I saw it in a movie."

"This ain't a movie!" April nearly shouted. "This is real life and you want to set the house we're in on fire? Are you two completely insane?"

"Every other possible decision and we die!" Cotton snapped. "There is no good option. This is the best of all the bad ideas we've got!"

April was quiet. She understood. Cotton knew she was right; this wasn't a movie. There would be no last-minute rescue, no magic twist at the end that would see them through this. Maybe the best they could hope for would be to die on their own terms.

Barnabas walked through the ranks and surveyed his men. It had taken a long time to build up this force, and it had not been easy. He thought back to how many he had discarded, for all manner of iniquity, but also for simply not meeting the height requirement.

He himself had been curious about that one and had even wondered aloud to God, but the answer had always been clear. This was what He wanted. This was what He needed His soldiers to be.

Despite those additional challenges, the building of this army had gone according to His will. Each man was now outfitted with a plate carrier provided by the U.S. military (from a National Guard armory they had raided), as well as a hammer and a sprinkling of knives. Firearms were forbidden.

This had also been a challenge, but Barnabas came to understand that the taking of life, and in particular the extensive slaughter they were about to be engaged in, was a very personal and sacrosanct thing. It would be blasphemy to use something as impersonal as a firearm to dispatch a soul from this earth.

Finally, he walked to Ezekiel 9. Blood splattered the man's face, and Barnabas saw his knife was bloody as well.

"I take it by your appearance that we delivered the message?"

"Yes, brother," Ezekiel 9 said.

There was something in his eyes. A hesitation.

"Say it, brother," Barnabas said. "Speak your mind."

"I do not think it will be enough, not to cow a man like this. I heard them talking and I saw the way he moved as I was leaving. We may need more."

"Leverage?" Barnabas asked.

"I believe what you say you have seen," Ezekiel 9 said. "That this man will be our undoing. If this is true, and I tell you what I have seen with my own eyes, a message will not be enough."

Barnabas thought about this for a moment.

"What do you propose?"

Roland stepped out of the Mercedes SUV he had acquired months before and, as always, appreciated the vehicle's relation to the military versions he had used in both Iraq and Afghanistan. He touched the hood and smiled, thinking back on those days and how well they had prepared him for what was to come.

He had changed out of his business attire and now wore his Crye combat pants, a t-shirt and a Ferro Concepts Slickster plate carrier that had seen better days.

A complement of his men unloaded from the other two vehicles, including Jorge and Brian. Roland walked to Jorge and looked the bigger man in the eyes.

"It's crunch time, hombre," Roland said. "Time to decide where you stand."

"Central Texas," Jorge said with a smile.

"My patience has a limit," Roland said. "Even for you. I need to know whose man you are."

"I'm my own man," Jorge said. "Always have been, even if you didn't know it. Randall Eisler understands that. I was always free to go."

"Man needs a group, particularly out here. How long you think you're gonna last on your own?"

"Until I don't," Jorge said flatly. "But it'll be my choice."

Roland set his jaw and then nodded.

"I ain't forgotten," Roland said. "What you did for me. All that time ago. But like I said, everything's got a limit."

Jorge didn't respond.

Roland turned to where Randall Eisler's men stood beside Harris Hawthorne's. He looked to the house and then back to the men.

"One fucking guy?" Roland shouted. "We're all out here standing on the Devil's backbone for one damn guy? I tell you what, that better be the freakin' Terminator himself in there."

"Pretty close," Bob said.

Harris looked at Bob for a moment and then back to Roland.

"There's something else," Harris said.

This caught Randall Eisler's attention.

"Something else?" Randall Eisler asked. He didn't like surprises.

. . .

Roland Reese scanned the field around him and then sighed. He turned back to the other men.

"Did we really all just walk into a trap?" Roland asked, the exasperation in his voice clear.

"Apparently, this is an evolving situation," Randall Eisler said.

"I feel like someone should have mentioned we might be surrounded by a hundred damn six-foot-tall cannibals who think they're on a mission from God!" Roland shouted.

"Sir," Harris said. "To be fair, we didn't have comms with you or with Randall Eisler, for that matter. We had to send a runner out just to get close enough for radio contact with Cypress Mill. No way we're going to reach Oatmeal. We also only understood the gravity of the situation very recently."

Roland wanted someone's head on a pike, but he also understood better than anyone how quickly things could change in the battle space.

"Okay," Roland said. "First things first. Let's address this guy in the house and then figure out which direction to go with the external threat."

Roland waved Randall over to him and then led the man away from the group.

"Your people take the vaccine yet?" Roland asked.

"Second group is getting it right now," Randall Eisler answered.

"How are you handling that?"

"Excommunication," Randall Eisler said simply. "We're going to do our best to be fair about it but can't have a bunch of hens in the fox house."

Roland smiled at this explanation. He had always appreciated Randall Eisler's strange sense of humor.

"How about you?" Randall Eisler asked. "How are you handling it?"

Roland locked eyes with Randall Eisler for a moment and then smiled.

"Different strokes for different folks," Roland said. "Know what I mean?"

"They know about that?" Randall Eisler asked.

"They will," Roland said. "It's a loyalty problem, you know what I mean? I get what you're doing and, of course, I will not interfere, but I can't have folks roaming around my area of operations who may have secret machinations against me. We'll see how it goes, and if they really do turn back, well..."

"Understood," Randall Eisler said.

Jesus, he thought to himself. *He's going to kill everyone who takes the vaccine.*

"Anyhow," Roland said and turned back to the house. "I think it's about time me and this man had a conversation."

"Hey there, you!" Roland shouted.

He had walked up the ravine and crossed into the front yard of the house. Now he stood out in front with no protection. He had even stripped off his plate carrier and left his pistol behind at the truck.

The truth was that he was not completely without protection. Jorge had moved to a small hill about five hundred meters out and set up with a sixteen-inch recce rifle and a solid 1-8x EOTech VUDU scope. If this man came out shooting, he was unlikely to get more than a round off before Jorge sent him to Valhalla.

"Come on out," Roland continued. "You can see me here. I ain't got nothing on me. No guns, no nothing. I just want to talk. See if we can work something out. Seems to me you're a man that can handle himself, so shouldn't be no problems with me being unarmed and all."

. . .

"What in the hell?" Cotton whispered as he walked to the window of the second-floor bedroom.

"Be careful!" April said quickly as she watched him walk into plain view.

"No," Cotton said and held up a hand. "I think I know this guy."

"What?" April asked.

"I could be wrong, but... yeah, I think I know him." Cotton unslung his rifle and held it beside him.

"What are you doing?" Jean asked.

"I'm going to talk to him."

"It could be a trap!" April said insistently.

"It's almost certainly a trap," Cotton agreed. "But I've still got the pistol and I won't go beyond the doorway."

There was a look approximating sheer terror on April's face. Cotton touched her shoulder.

"It's fine," he said. "If this guy is who I think he is, we might just have a chance."

"What if he isn't?" April asked.

"The plan stays the same." He looked out the window to where the sun was slowly dropping out of the sky. "You'll just have to hold them off until the sun goes down and then you light this place up."

"We'll do it," Jean said firmly. "You don't have to worry."

Cotton looked at her.

"I don't, Fancy Face." He walked back to the window and stopped. "I'm coming out!"

Cotton stopped at the bottom of the stairs and turned to the short entryway that led to the front door. He took the walk to the door and sat his rifle beside the doorframe. If things went south, he could retrieve it quickly and get on target.

He reached over and partially pulled the curtain obscuring the front window open. Just enough to let his eyes acclimate to the change in light so he wouldn't be momentarily blind when he opened the door.

Roland waited patiently. He had seen movement through the second-floor window and he thought there was a reasonable possibility that this man was going to come out. After that, he wasn't quite sure what direction things would go. By all accounts, this one man had so far killed a half dozen of Harris' men.

Most of those men had no actual military experience, but they had still trained a lot and should have at least put up some semblance of a fight. Even Roland had to admit that a lot of the training civilians had been receiving in the last few years before the virus was pretty damn good. Sometimes, it was even better than what he had gotten because there was no inbred doctrine declaring how everything should be done.

That was part of why civilian groups like the FPAR had given the military so much trouble during the brief flare up of what they could only call a revolutionary war. The civilians had an advantage in their ability to be free thinkers and more quickly adapt to changing circumstances.

Roland watched the front door crack open. There was a moment of hesitation and then it opened fully, and a man stepped onto the front porch. He was smart, Roland thought. He was staying close to the door. No doubt he had an AR ready to go inside.

Roland narrowed his eyes for a moment and then even leaned forward a bit on the balls of his feet.

"Son-of-a-bitch," Cotton said under his breath.

. . .

"Holy shit!" Roland Reese shouted. "Senior Chief Wiley!"

"Master Chief Reese," Cotton said, unable to hold back a smile. "What in the hell are you doing out here?"

"I'm from here!" Roland retorted. "What in the hell are you doing out here?"

Cotton surveyed the horizon behind Roland and then looked back to him.

"Can I assume that if I step off this porch, the sniper you've undoubtedly got out there won't blow my head off?"

Roland held up a hand and made a quick 'cutting' motion, signaling to Jorge to make his weapon safe and head in.

"He would have done it too," Roland said. "Former Unit guy. Shoot the balls off a mosquito at five hundred meters."

Cotton walked down the steps and toward Roland, yet still stopped well beyond striking distance. He trusted this man, but not that much.

"You're the King, aren't you?" Cotton asked.

"That's what everyone keeps telling me," Roland said with a nod. "Why ain't you in West Virginia?"

"Remember the last thing you said to me?" Cotton asked.

"Run," Roland replied.

"So, I did. Plan is to run as far north as I can."

"Alaska?" Roland asked.

Cotton wasn't quite ready to show all of his cards.

"Hard to say. Deep north Canada might be the safest bet, if we can get there."

"Go where people aren't, right?" Roland surmised. "Make the cold your first line of defense."

"That's about the size of it."

"Shit, Cotton," Roland said, and his voice changed. "It's all scorched earth."

"What are you talking about?"

"I have comms with the cities. They count on me and others like me around the country to keep some semblance of order out here. Latest word is the Russians are camped out at the northern border. They took Canada and Alaska. Even if you could make a go of it in Alaska, you'd never get there."

"I can try," Cotton said.

"You'll fail. I'm telling you this as a friend."

Cotton paused for a moment.

"Why aren't the Russians moving south?"

"Country's full of damn cannibals," Roland said

with a shrug. "They're just playing a waiting game. No reason to invade and lose maybe millions of fighters when they can just wait us out."

Cotton didn't know what to say. He also wasn't sure what Roland's game was here, but he couldn't think of a reason the man would lie to him about this. It was just too big.

"So, we'll go somewhere else," Cotton said. "But the obvious question is: are you going to let us walk out of here?"

"Of course I am," Roland said. "Hell man, if I'd known it was you, none of this would be happening in the first place."

"Because you're the King of Texas now," Cotton said with a smile.

"Central Texas at least," Roland said. "It took a hell of a lot of killing to get this far, but we're making a go of it."

"I knew it was one of us," Cotton said. "When I heard about that shot from two miles away. Had to be us or Army Special Missions Unit. Maybe that Canadian sniper from JTF2 who took that crazy shot in Iraq. Only a handful of guys in the world could have made a shot like that. And way I heard it, you made it three times. On moving targets."

Roland laughed.

"Come on, man. You know how those shots go. That was mostly luck. Unlikely I could do it again."

"Why did you?" Cotton asked. "Why did you kill the President?"

Roland looked at him hard for a moment.

"Remember all his talk?" Roland asked. "Remember how he said he was gonna turn things around, make things right again? Put them back the way they were?"

"Yeah," Cotton said.

"He was gonna do it. I believed that to my core. I didn't vote for the son-of-a-bitch, but I believed he was going to do what he said."

Cotton understood.

"And you didn't want that."

"We're hunters, Cotton. War was winding down, and we were spending more time training than we were hunting bad guys. How long you think it would have been before I drank myself to death? Or you messed up your gig teaching CQB at the command?"

He wasn't wrong. Cotton knew it.

"So, you shot the President and pulled the plug on civilization," Cotton concluded.

"We were never civilized," Roland said. "Doesn't matter, anyway. It's done. Now the question I propose to you is: do you want in?"

"In on what?" Cotton asked.

"This," Roland said. "A man like you, you can write your own ticket out here if you know the right people. Shit, look how many folks showed up just to root you out of this house."

"And you'd let me stay human?" Cotton asked.

"Well," Roland said slowly, "we'd have to discuss that."

"Ain't nothing to discuss," Cotton said. "If you're gonna let me walk, let me walk, but I'm not for sale."

Roland looked as if he had another argument chambered when a voice came up from the ravine.

"We've got company!"

April intently watched the conversation going on outside. She noticed Cotton had left the porch. He did indeed know this man.

Jean looked at her watch and then at the sun again.

"I'm going downstairs," Jean said. "Pull out the lighter fluid and get it ready."

"But he knows him," April protested. "I think it might be okay."

"Maybe," Jean said. "But if it goes south, I don't want to be scrambling."

"No," April said. "I'll do it."

Jean looked confused.

"Why?" She asked.

"If something happens out there," April said, "you're a better shot. Hell, you're a better fighter. It's better if you're watching his back."

Jean understood.

"I won't be long," April said.

Both Harris and Randall Eisler came walking up the ravine toward Cotton and Roland.

Cotton took a step back and his hand moved to the grip of his Glock 17.

"No!" Roland barked. "They're no threat to you!"

Harris and Randall Eisler had both stopped in their tracks but then relaxed a bit as Cotton relaxed his right hand.

"Lookout called in that there are about a dozen of them lined up on the road to the east, about two thousand meters out," Harris said.

"A dozen what?" Cotton asked.

Roland sighed.

"There's something else we should discuss," Roland said. "There's another faction out there, not quite as agreeable as we are. Kind of a religious cult of cannibals."

"Like, out there in the world?" Cotton asked.

"No, out here with us."

"Fantastic," Cotton said sarcastically.

"All the more reason to throw in, at least for the time being," Roland said. "Give it kind of a test run."

"How many are there?" Cotton asked.

Roland looked to Harris.

"Best I can figure we're probably looking at a hundred strong," Harris said.

"Are you kidding me?" Cotton asked.

"And they're all over six feet tall," Roland added.

Cotton laughed.

"No, seriously," Roland went on. "It's some kind of selection process they have."

"We're surrounded by one hundred six-foot-tall cannibals?"

"Over six feet tall," Harris interjected. "Not just six feet tall."

"That's about the size of it," Roland agreed. "And the only way out is through. So, I say again, will you join us? It's the only way in hell we're all getting out of this mess in one piece."

. . .

Jean watched the conversation going on in the front yard. More men had joined her father, and it at least seemed like they were getting on okay. If her father knew this man, maybe, just maybe they were going to walk away from this.

Jean stopped this train of thought and turned to the doorway that opened up to the second-floor landing. April had been gone for several minutes, and Jean hadn't heard a thing.

She walked to the door and looked down the stairs.

"April?" She called out.

No answer.

Jean walked down the stairs. It was possible the woman hadn't heard her, but all the same, she drew the Glock 19 and held it at the ready. Every plank on the staircase seemed to creak beneath her. She stopped at the bottom. Was this the wrong play? Should she be calling her father in?

She shook her head.

No, then he'd go back to treating her like a child again.

She walked into the living room and turned to face the kitchen. Through the doorway, she saw April. The woman was tied to a chair with tape over her mouth. Her eyes were wild with fear.

Jean started to bring her gun up but felt it being snatched away from her at the same moment that a pair of powerful hands pressed heavy tape over her mouth. She tried to scream, but the sound was stifled.

They surrounded her. One man grabbed her legs while another tried to get hold of her flailing arms. For a moment, just a moment, she panicked.

Then everything snapped into focus. She felt her heart rate drop and slowed her breathing. Her right hand dropped to the knife on her belt. She drew it, turned her body and struck, not blindly but at the face her eyes had found.

The cannibal known as Numbers 12 stumbled back, furiously grasping at the knife in his throat as his blood sprayed across the room. Out of the corner of her eye, Jean could see April thrashing wildly in her chair. She was trying to break free, but with little success.

"Two is one, one is none," Cotton had always said. Jean had taken this advice to heart.

Her left hand slid into her left front pocket and retrieved the smaller folding knife. Now a heavy arm locked around her throat, cutting off her air supply. He was trying to choke her. She flipped open the knife and slashed at the arm in question. It instantly released its grip on her. Jean also felt the man holding her legs let go. She hit the floor with a thud.

It was so quiet. Why was it so quiet?

Jean leapt to her feet and realized why it was so quiet. These men had all taped their own mouths shut to avoid any accidental noises.

For a split second, she considered ripping the tape off of her own mouth so that she could scream for help, but by the time she did so, they would be on her and it would be over. She only had one shot at survival.

Violence of action.

Jean turned and threw the hardest sidekick of her life into the knee of the man closest to her, just as he was reaching out for her. Every ligament in his knee snapped with a sickening sound that reverberated off the walls.

"Go after the weak points," her father had said. "Eyes, throat, knees. Don't kick them in the balls, you'll miss. Everyone does. You won't be a match for a full-grown man when it comes to strength. You have to fight dirty. That's the only way you walk away."

Her hand gripped the folding knife as a second man grabbed at her. He was scared. She could see it.

He wasn't committing himself to the attack because he had already seen what happened to his friends.

He paid for this hesitancy with his life. Jean screamed fruitlessly beneath the tape over her mouth as she lunged and drove the folding knife into his left eye. She felt electric as her body whipped forward and she drove every ounce of strength into the strike.

His light went out like someone had thrown a switch and his body crumpled to the floor.

Jean felt hands on her again, trying to restrain her like they had the first time. She spun and lashed out with her knife, but this time, they were ready. Three of them pinned her to the floor, and she only had a moment to appreciate how dire her situation was before the darkness came.

Ezekiel 9 slowed his breathing down and turned to Numbers 7 and Genesis 20. He motioned to them that he would take her back through the way they had come, through the hole in the wall inside the pantry.

They were to stay and finish off the woman, then follow him.

.   .   .

"So," Cotton said. "Should I trust the savages I know over the savages I don't?"

As he was saying this, another man emerged from the tall grass holding a recce rifle with a scope on it. It was Jorge, who had been acting as Roland's sniper on the hill.

"We ain't no savages!" Harris countered. "We always do things as civilized as we can."

"I saw your little horror show in the storm cellar," Cotton said. "That's what you call civil?"

"Storm cellar?" Harris asked. "We ain't never been in the storm cellar. That thing's been chained shut as long as I can remember."

Cotton's mind flashed back to the bodies in the storm cellar, then to Ralph stabbed to death in the kitchen.

They had come up from the storm cellar.

He drew a sudden breath, turned and bolted for the door. Roland picked up on his old teammate's cue and ran behind him. Jorge followed suit; the reflexes of men who have assaulted hundreds of structures kicked in.

Cotton's Glock 17 was already out of the holster as he barreled through the front door and into the living room. There were two bodies on the floor, one with a knife buried in his throat. It was Jean's knife.

Cotton turned to the kitchen and saw them. There were three men, one of them with a knife to April's throat.

Despite the adrenaline surge and the terror he felt at the idea that his daughter might be dead, Cotton performed a smooth press of the trigger and put a round between the eyes of the man holding the knife. The cannibal dropped like a pile of bricks. The other two cannibals turned and moved toward the pantry door.

Cotton felt a round zip past his head and nail one of the two cannibals in the back of the skull. In a moment, Cotton was on top of the last remaining man and threw him to the ground. He was a big boy, but no match for Cotton Wiley.

Cotton pressed the muzzle of his pistol to the man's forehead.

"I am prepared to die for my savior," the man said.

"Who said anything about dying?" Cotton asked as he drew his Winkler fixed blade and drove it hard into the man's right shoulder. The man screamed and Cotton twisted. "You got a long time coming before you die, son. Where's my daughter!"

Cotton drew the knife out and positioned it at the man's groin.

"I'll do it! I'll cut 'em off!" Cotton shouted. "You know I will!"

"The pantry!" The man replied in a panic and pointed with his good arm. "Ezekiel 9 took her into the tunnels!"

Cotton put the pistol back to the man's forehand and pressed the trigger. The Nephilim's head bounced against the floor as his blood splattered the tile.

"I need a second!" Cotton shouted as he dropped his NODs and moved to the pantry door.

"Go!" Roland said and pointed to Jorge. "It's his daughter."

"I'm on it," Jorge said as he set down his rifle and drew his pistol.

Roland ran to the door of the house.

"I need NODs for Jorge! Now!"

One man who had come with him scampered down the side of the ravine and within two minutes was back up the side holding a ballistic helmet with a set of DTNVS mounted to it.

"What in the hell is going on in there?" Harris asked, but they ignored his question as the man who had retrieved the NODs sprinted past and up the steps, where he handed them off to Roland.

Roland walked into the living room and threw

the helmet to Jorge, who put it on and headed for the pantry door that Cotton had already disappeared through. Jorge walked into the pantry and saw what had happened. There was a hole in the wall, and inside of that wall was another hole in the floor.

"No way this ends well," Jorge muttered as he lowered himself through the hole and dropped into the storm cellar.

Inside the cellar was almost complete darkness, with only slivers of ambient light coming in through the storm cellar doors. He lowered the DTNVS and powered them up, illuminating the room in a blueish white.

Jorge turned and saw Cotton at the far end of the cellar standing next to an old wooden shelf piled high with random junk. The Nephilim had pulled it to the side, and it revealed a man-sized tunnel into the wall.

"You've got to be kidding me," Jorge said.

Cotton held up a hand to Jorge and pointed into the tunnel. Jorge gave a thumbs up and the two men moved forward.

In all the excitement there had been no time to cut April loose from the chair that the Nephilim had bound her to. Roland Reese took a knee, opened his Gerber knife and cut her free. Once April's hands were no longer restrained she pulled the tape from her mouth and took a deep breath.

"You're okay," Roland assured her. "I got you."

April looked to the pantry door that Cotton and Jorge had disappeared through.

"You're worried about the girl?" Roland asked. "Cotton's daughter Jean?"

April was surprised.

"You know her?" April asked.

Roland smiled.

"From a long time ago," he said and then caught himself. "Well, maybe not that long ago. Just feels like another life, but yeah. Me and Cotton go way back."

April nodded.

"And we been through way worse than this," Roland said.

By now, several of the men had filtered up the edge of the ravine and were standing in the front yard. More of Barnabas' followers had been spotted around the property and the tension among the men was increasing.

"What in the hell are they doing in there?" Harris asked.

"We'll give 'em another minute," Randall Eisler said, but he had already retrieved his own carbine from the truck.

Bob looked around and then turned to Randall Eisler.

"You hear that?" Bob asked.

Randall Eisler scanned the perimeter and then shook his head.

"What do you hear?" He asked.

"Nothing," Bob said. "No birds, no crickets, no nothing."

"Shit," Harris said. "He's right."

As if on cue, a torch lit in the semi-darkness of the field. Then another. Then another. Then torch after torch after torch. They circled the perimeter.

"Jesus," Harris gasped.

"That's a hell of a lot more than a hundred," Randall Eisler said. He turned to the house and shouted. "We have a problem out here!"

CHAPTER 10

ROLAND WALKED out of the house and stopped on the porch. He couldn't believe what he was seeing. There were easily two hundred torches out in the fields. This was far more than he had bargained for when he hopped in that truck with Jorge.

"We're surrounded," Randall Eisler said and brass checked his AR to ensure a round was in the chamber.

"Good," Roland Reese said. One of his men walked up and handed him an AR. "That means we can fight in any direction."

Randall Eisler knew the quote Roland had appropriated. It was from a World War Two era Marine named Lewis B. "Chesty" Puller. In that moment, he understood that there was a reason

Roland Reese had captured all of central Texas under his banner, and it had nothing to do with luck.

"Are you insane?" Harris shouted. "We have to get out of here!"

"There's nowhere to run," Roland said bluntly.

Harris understood, and he knew he had to get himself in check. He had always secretly wanted a fight like this, an opportunity to really prove himself. More importantly, he needed to prove to himself that he wasn't the coward he always secretly feared he would become when the zero-hour struck. Even if the plan was for him and Bob to round up the boys and sneak out the back once the fighting started.

"Okay," Harris said. "You're right. We're going to make a stand."

"Damn right," Roland said with a smile.

The sun had fully descended from the sky and the torches were the only thing lighting up the night. Then they dimmed. Every torch suddenly went out.

"A little psy-ops," Randall Eisler surmised. He took a knee and brought his weapon up to the ready. "They're coming."

Most of the men did the same, but Roland remained standing. He spat on the ground and brought his weapon up.

"I don't kneel for no man," Roland said.

"Good luck with that," Randall Eisler replied, and remained in his half-kneeling firing position.

"They won't have guns," Bob said. "Barnabas thinks it's blasphemy. They'll mostly have hammers, maybe some knives."

It sounded like a moan, but more guttural. Perhaps it more approximated a growl, but it came in a wave, multitudes of voices growling. Then the men saw the tops of heads coming at them through the tall grass.

"Hold fast," Roland said. "Wait until they're in the open. That's how we're going to get them. Shoot too soon and they'll just disappear back out there."

There was about one hundred feet of standoff distance between where the men stood and the border of the tall grass. Roland knew that if they caught enough of the Nephilim in the open before they started firing, it would be like shooting fish in a barrel.

The first of the Nephilim emerged. His white eyes were wild, lips pulled back from yellow teeth, and he held what looked like a full-size sledgehammer. Then another came and another until there were dozens thundering across the crackling dead grass.

"Hold!" Roland shouted.

Randall Eisler's thumb rested on the safety selector of his AR. He could feel his breathing speeding up, but he knew that wouldn't help him, so he slowed it back down again. He put the red dot of his Holosun on the head of the Nephilim most directly in his line of sight, ready to shift from that man to the next as fast as he could acquire the target.

"Hold!" Roland shouted again.

They were very close.

How long is he going to wait? Randall Eisler wondered to himself.

"Kill these motherfuckers!" Roland roared.

Weapons began firing and Randall Eisler watched with quite a bit of satisfaction as the round he fired knocked back the Nephilim coming toward him. He didn't quite hit the man in the head, but the chest would do just as well.

The rest of the men were doing the same, hitting center mass and quickly transitioning to the next target. Randall Eisler could see men performing immediate action drills on their firearms, already having problems with jams. It was the cheap steel case ammo they were using, and probably some sub-par weapons.

Then he saw something that shook him. Through his red dot sight, he watched one of the

Nephilim who had been gunned down slowly pull himself to an upright position and look right at him.

"Can't be," Randall Eisler said to himself. "Can't be."

He put his red dot on the resurrected Nephilim's head, let out a breath, slowly pulled his trigger and put the round right where it needed to be between the giant cannibal's eyes. This time, he went down and stayed down.

Then he saw other Nephilim doing the same thing, crawling to an upright position and then standing. They were all doing it.

"They're coming back!" Randall Eisler shouted. "They ain't staying dead!"

In an instant, Roland saw what he was talking about. The piles of dead men just feet from them were getting back to standing.

He understood. Even if it made no sense, it made more sense than zombies.

"Plates!" Roland shouted. "They've got plates! Head shots! Now!"

It was too late. The wave of resurrected Nephilim crashed into the group of men and began attacking them with hammers and knives, caving in skulls and slashing throats with a level of skill perfected in scores of previous encounters. They had never been in a battle as large as this, but they were still not found wanting.

Amid the chaos, Harris found Bob and patted him on the shoulder.

"It's time!" Harris said.

Bob understood.

Harris turned to Roland.

"They're in the ravine, I need to get re-enforcements down there!"

Roland knew they were surrounded and also understood that if they came up out of the ravine, it would become a big problem quickly.

"Okay, go!" Roland directed.

Harris couldn't suppress a smile as he began grabbing his men and directing them into the ravine.

Inside the house, April watched in horror as the men were being slaughtered by these giants. She picked up her AR and checked the chamber. She was going to have to fight, whether she wanted to or not.

Cotton walked through the tunnel with his weapon at the ready. He reached up and clicked on the Sure-fire scout light attached to his helmet, set to infrared.

Since they had left the cellar and its ambient light, the tunnel had grown progressively darker until it was pitch black. Even the best NODs needed at least some ambient light to function. In the absence of that, IR light would work as well.

He wondered how long ago they had dug out this tunnel. Thus far, he and Jorge had traveled a few hundred feet. How far could this possibly go?

He was also curious about the man behind him. Roland had referred to him being in Delta. If that was true, it meant Cotton could trust him on a job like this, but how far could he really trust him? This wouldn't be a good time to find out, but he also had no choice.

Ezekiel 9 emerged from the tunnel exit with the unconscious young girl slung over his shoulder. He was still in the tunnel complex itself and one more turn brought him into the outer chamber where Barnabas had given him the knife and sent him on his mission. He had returned alone with the girl, the rest of his men almost certainly dead. Would Barnabas see this as failure?

Ahead of him he saw a lamp light and moved toward it until he emerged into the fresh air. Here he found Barnabas, with several other men gathered together. Barnabas turned to him. He smiled. It was not a failure.

"You have her," Barnabas said. "His daughter."

"Yes, brother," Ezekiel 9 said. "But I am certain he is behind me in the tunnel. He may not be alone."

"I see," Barnabas said. "Then lay her down, brother. You know what you must do."

Ezekiel 9 lay Jean down on the dead grass and stood back up. He drew his knife from where it had been stowed in his belt.

"Alone?" He asked.

Barnabas considered this for a moment and turned to the men who had gathered with him. He indicated six who were standing together and waved them toward Ezekiel 9.

"This man," Barnabas said. "He ends us. I have seen it, but that does not mean it must come to pass."

Ezekiel 9 nodded.

"I will not fail you."

Roland slammed the stock of his rifle into the head of the attacking Nephilim, then spun the rifle around and took the point-blank shot he was offered directly into the cannibal's head. He worked the CMC trigger of his rifle like a master violinist would use his instrument and executed three more within three meters of him.

The rest of the men were not fairing as well. It was mostly hand-to-hand combat, knives and elbows being used just as frequently as rifles and pistols. He looked to his left and saw more Nephilim coming up out of the ravine. They must have overtaken the men Harris had moved there.

"Fall back!" Roland shouted. "Into the house!"

April heard the shout and knew it was time to act. She smashed out the window in the small hallway with the butt of her rifle, took up a half kneeling position and began taking shots at the advancing Nephilim. True to her word, she was hitting her targets up this close, and she was buying enough time for Roland and his men to move to the house.

April kept up a steady rate of fire and suddenly felt her bolt lock back on an empty chamber. It took a moment to process that she had gone through her entire magazine, but once she did; her left hand snatched another mag out of her left back pocket, slammed it into the magazine well and sent the bolt forward. No sooner was the round chambered than she got back on target and started her steady staccato rhythm of 5.56 rounds chewing through Nephilim flesh.

The men were streaming inside until the last one entered and slammed the door behind him.

Roland Reese locked the door and looked down at April.

"Thank you," he said.

"Thank me after you get us out of this," April replied.

The desperation in her eyes was clear. It wasn't just a smart-ass remark. It was a request.

Roland looked around the lower floor of the house. It was dark.

"It's too dark in here!" He called out. "Light some lanterns but turn them down low. Just enough so we can see."

Daniel 4 watched the mayhem surrounding the house from his post with Barnabas on the hilltop. The girl lay at their feet, still passed out. Barnabas wondered if Ezekiel 9 may have struck her too hard. The purpose behind her abduction had been for her value as leverage over her father, should it come to that. This was obviously not possible if she was dead.

Barnabas watched his flock surrounding the

house, still well over one hundred strong. Despite the use of the plate carriers and the protection they provided, there had still been heavy losses. It would be worth it, though. Judging by the sheer number of the unsaved he had seen at the house, it was unlikely that they had left their communities very well defended.

For quite some time, the Nephilim had been using the storm cellar of the house as a killing room and storage site for meat. He understood that this man Harris had also been using the house itself as a lure, never aware that anyone else was there, as the Nephilim moved mostly through the tunnels below the house.

Barnabas had seen a potential there to eventually exterminate Harris and his group once it became large enough. Much like a master gardener, he would let them grow until the time was right that they should reap the whirlwind. Then this stranger had arrived with his daughter and the other woman, so Barnabas let the scenario play out.

Then the Lord delivered to him the vision of this man ending him and was told that it could not pass. Then the other sinners came. It was almost as if this house was some sort of magnet, a powerful magnet pulling in all these sinners for the culling. So, Barnabas would be the one to do the culling of these unclean swine.

"We could set the house ablaze," Daniel 4 suggested. "We would not lose any more of our men that way."

Barnabas looked at him with disgust.

"Have you forgotten so soon?" Barnabas demanded.

Daniel 4 instantly understood.

It would be blasphemy. The Lord required a blood sacrifice performed by His servants with their own hands. Not by fire.

"Of course," Daniel 4 replied.

"Hm."

Barnabas turned and looked back at the entrance to the tunnels. He wondered how long it would take Ezekiel 9 and his brothers to attend to just one man.

Cotton slowed down and clicked off his IR light for a moment. He could still see. Not perfectly, but there was light ahead. They were getting closer to some kind of a light source, possibly an exit. He turned and looked back at Jorge.

Jorge responded with a thumbs up. He had his Colt 1911 pistol by his side. There was no red dot on it, so he would not have an aiming device in the darkness, but the upside to fighting in close quarters like this was that aiming wasn't as much of a problem as it might be shooting out in the open.

Cotton took a step forward and stopped. Was it his imagination or did he hear footsteps? The two men had come to a curve in the tunnel, effectively a blind turn.

Damn it, Cotton thought to himself. *Why here?*

Cotton signaled that he was about to move to the left where he would hug the wall and "pie" around the blind curve. This would give him some reaction time versus hugging the inside of the turn, where his only option would be to walk directly into anyone that might be coming.

Then he stopped. What if there were more outside? If he started shooting and they had Jean, they would hear him coming a mile away and either kill her or run. Neither of those was an acceptable outcome.

He turned to Jorge and made a show of holstering his Glock. He drew his Winkler fixed blade in an overhead grip. Jorge understood, and Cotton watched him also holster his weapon and pull a dagger from his belt.

They would have to do this quietly. Like gentlemen used to.

Cotton moved around the corner in a wide hook and saw the first of the Nephilim. He was only feet from him and tape covered his mouth.

The cannibal lunged at Cotton and the former SEAL responded by swinging his knife hand like a haymaker, and drove the blade so hard into the man's left temple that it was buried to the hilt and the tip exited from the other side. It was overkill, and he knew it. Seeing one of the cannibals who had taken his daughter enraged him, and he was now rewarded for this emotional outburst by being unable to retrieve his knife from the man's head.

In an instant, two of the Nephilim were on top of him, first pinning him to the ground and then delivering blows. One of the first blows activated the breakaway feature on his Wilcox mount and sent his night vision flying across the tunnel. Now he was just as blind as they were. He could only hope that Jorge was faring better.

Jorge closed with the first Nephilim within reach and made quick work of him. He could see that Cotton was on the ground fighting and that someone had knocked his NODs off, but there was nothing he could do about it. He had his own problems.

That's why I always disable that dumb ass break-away feature, Jorge thought to himself.

Two more of the big cannibals were now on top of him, but he knew they couldn't see him. They were fighting blind. He took advantage of this and side stepped their clumsy attack. He then lunged back at them with two quick strikes of the Fairbarn-Sykes fighting knife and cut each man's throat in turn.

He watched them in the illumination of the white phosphor tubes, clawing in panic at their throats as they bled out in the darkness.

Cotton locked one of the Nephilim between his legs in a Brazilian Jiu-Jitsu guard. It wasn't an ideal position to fight from, but at least he had control of the man. One advantage of BJJ in the dark was that you could feel your way to the attack. There was no need to see.

He felt a knife slash dangerously close to his face and responded by extending his hips to push the trapped man further from him, and then spun onto his side, upending the man and putting him closer to the cannibal that Cotton could feel was to his left. He felt the reverberation of a hammer striking the ground beside him. The Nephilim knew he was there and was striking blindly.

Cotton reached out, found the cannibal's leg and pulled him to the ground. Without hesitation, he turned back to the Nephilim he had trapped and used his legs to pull him in tight to him, effectively capturing him in a bear hug. His left hand slid out along the man's right arm until he found the knife and wrenched it free.

He didn't repeat his last knife fighting mistake, and instead took three quick strikes into the man's head and then released him. From there, he rolled onto all fours and sprang forward to where he knew the man he had pulled to the ground would be.

In a split-second, Cotton was on top of him.

"Die motherfucker!" Cotton hissed quietly as he stabbed furiously at the fallen man.

"Stop," Jorge said quietly from behind him. "He's dead. We have to move."

Cotton looked up into the darkness and could just barely see something being held in front of his face. He reached out and took it. Jorge had retrieved his NODs.

. . .

"Okay!" Roland shouted as he moved through the house. "Everyone on a window. If you know how to set up interlocking fields of fire, do it! Don't be shy about sticking your head out, these guys don't have firepower."

The Nephilim had drawn back into the darkness of the tall grass, far enough that the men inside couldn't take potshots at them.

Brian stood with Randall Eisler in the living room, watching the men square away their fighting positions. He had barely slept in the last twenty-four hours, but could feel the adrenaline surging through his body.

"What do you think they're gonna do?" Brian asked.

"Charge the house, scorched earth style," Randall Eisler replied. "At least, that's what I would do."

"That would be suicide!" Brian said.

"No," Randall Eisler replied. "What we're doing is suicide. They've still got at least a hundred damn fighters out there. What are we down to, you think? Maybe thirty? If that?"

Brian looked around. The man was right.

"We're trapped like rats in a damn cage," Randall

Eisler said. "And my guess is at some point Mister King of Texas over there is going to tell us we're going to have to fight to the last man. Ain't no other way."

"There has to be!" Brian protested.

"What?"

"Another way!"

Randall Eisler smiled.

"You work on that, son. Let me know what you come up with."

Cotton had re-attached and adjusted his night vision and begun moving forward with Jorge. This time, he let the big man take the lead. Cotton had the distinct impression that this was not the former Unit member's first time navigating his way through a tunnel like this.

Jorge held up an open hand to stop Cotton. He leaned forward a bit and seemed to look at something. He drew his knife again and pointed forward, then held up three fingers. Jorge then gestured to his night vision and motioned upward.

Cotton understood. He hit the release button on his Wilcox mount and lifted his night vision into the fully stowed position. They were about to get some light and it wouldn't make sense to still be using night vision.

The two men moved forward into the outer chamber of the tunnel complex and now Cotton saw what Jorge had. There were three sentries standing there, but none had yet seen them. Jorge stopped Cotton again and held up three fingers. Then he dropped one, so two remained.

It was go time.

Jorge dropped one more finger.

Cotton gripped his knife. This had to be fast, and it had to be quiet. He knew that he needed to control himself. He couldn't freak out again like he had back in the tunnel.

Jorge dropped the last finger.

Execute.

Both men moved quickly and quietly, killing the three Nephilim in the outer chamber. One was able to get out a stifled shout, but Cotton thought it was unlikely the noise would reach the outside.

Jorge did a quick check of the bodies but found no other weapons aside from the hammers the Nephilim carried. He stood up and motioned to Cotton that they should move forward. Cotton nodded and followed.

. . .

"Why are they just standing there?" April asked. She stood at the second-floor window with Roland watching the Nephilim that had encircled the house. Just a minute earlier, they had moved out of the tall grass again.

They didn't move. Not a muscle.

Roland had not given the order to start shooting, as it felt like some kind of trap.

"I don't know," Roland replied. "But I don't like it."

Randall Eisler came in the door to the second-floor bedroom they were in.

"All positions are set," Randall Eisler said. "If they come at us, we're gonna give 'em a hell of a fight."

Roland didn't like how that sounded.

"Is it a fight we'll win?"

"Depends on your definition of the word 'win,'" Randall Eisler replied.

"We walk away from this," Roland clarified.

"Oh," Randall Eisler replied. "Yeah, probably not."

"What is that?" April asked and pointed to a light that had just appeared on a hill in the distance.

Roland leaned forward to get a better look. Then he noticed something else. The Nephilim were all turning to look at the light. In the midst of this, one of them lit a torch and held it high.

"No way is that good," Roland muttered.

A slow growl erupted from the gathered throngs of giant cannibals, and then, moving as if they were a wave of fury upon an ocean of death, they ran forward and crashed into the house.

Jean Wiley felt her eyes flutter, and in an instant, she realized she was awake. She opened her eyes, but just barely. Just enough to see what was directly ahead of her, or in this case, above her.

There were two men, both of them very large, and they were almost certainly cannibals. She was lying at their feet.

She closed her eyes completely again and worked to control her breathing. Her father was coming for her. She knew it. When he did, she had to be ready.

"I gave the signal," Daniel 4 said as he dropped the spent torch to the ground. "Soon everyone in the house will be dead."

"Good," Barnabas said. "This has been an expensive victory, but a necessary one. After we have regrouped, we will head for Cypress Mill."

"Tonight?" Daniel 4 asked.

Barnabas turned to him. It was not anger in his eyes. It was disappointment.

"Do you desire a rest, brother, after all of your work?"

"No," Daniel 4 said quickly. "It's not that. I just think the men may be tired. It may be good to attend to the wounded."

Barnabas reached out and put a hand on Daniel 4's shoulder. Barnabas was taller than his second in command, by a full four inches. He smiled at him.

"Do you feel the need to question me?" Barnabas asked. "Is there something within you that cries out to lead?"

"No," Daniel 4 said quickly. "It's just—"

Barnabas pulled the smaller man into him with his left hand as he struck with his right, burying the knife that he had secreted behind his back into Daniel 4's chest.

"It's okay," Barnabas said. "Ask for forgiveness. Ask me for forgiveness and it shall be granted."

Daniel 4 looked up at his leader as blood spilled from his mouth.

"You... aren't God," Daniel 4 choked the

words out.

"Aren't I?" Barnabas asked. "Who do these men follow? I think, perhaps... I am as close to God as you will ever get."

Barnabas pulled the knife from Daniel 4's chest and struck again, this time deep into the man's heart. He knelt as Daniel 4 fell to the ground and lay him beside the girl. She would be next.

Then he saw movement out of the corner of his eye. He knew who it was. It could be no one else. Barnabas snatched up the girl and stood, pulling her against him. She began fighting, and he gripped her neck hard enough that it should have broken. This slowed her struggle. He put the blade of his knife to her throat and she stopped moving.

Then he saw them clearly. Two men moving toward him, both with pistols raised.

"Stop!" Barnabas shouted. "I will kill her!"

Cotton and Jorge slowed to a stop, but kept their weapons up.

"Let her go and you can walk away," Cotton called out. "I got no quarrel with you. I just want my daughter back."

"Perhaps I have a quarrel with you," Barnabas shot back. "How many of my followers have you killed this night?"

"Only the ones that needed killin'," Cotton replied.

Barnabas laughed.

"How very Texan of you," Barnabas said. "Is that what this is? Typical Texan hubris?"

"Call it what you want," Cotton said. "But if she dies, you die."

Cotton watched Jean's hand moving slowly up the front of her shirt.

What in the hell are you playing at girl? Cotton thought to himself. Then he understood. Her eyes were locked on his.

"I came here from Arkansas," Barnabas said. "I never cared much for Texans, but I knew you would be easy to manipulate, because you're followers by nature."

"Not sure how much more of this shit I can take," Jorge whispered.

"Hold fast," Cotton replied. He knew he had no option. Barnabas was keeping his head behind Jean's, crouching down to shield himself.

"And here we see this Texan hubris in full effect. The idea that just two of you would come here for me when I have an entire army at my right hand?"

"You sure think highly of yourself," Cotton said.

"I've spent so long!" Barnabas shouted. "Searching! Waiting! Waiting for the second coming, for the return of the Lord. Preparing the land for Him! I've spent so long searching that I never saw what was right in front of me."

Jean's hand gripped the small dagger that was secured in the scabbard that hung around her neck. She felt the tug of the 550 cord on the back of her neck and the 'click' as she pulled the knife free from the kydex sheathe.

She could feel the man's grip relaxing as he talked. Her moment was coming.

"Perhaps it is I, who am the Lord," Barnabas said, his face twisted into a sick smile at his own revelation.

Jean looked into her father's eyes.

I love you; she mouthed.

Cotton wanted to say something, to stop her, but he knew there was no other way.

In one movement, Jean slammed her heel down on the top of Barnabas' foot and drove her left elbow into his ribs. It wasn't enough to break his grip, but it was enough for her to turn herself around and violently drive the dagger up into his sternum, piercing his diaphragm muscle.

Barnabas stumbled back and grasped at the dagger in his belly. It was clear that he couldn't breathe. His eyes were wild with disbelief. How had this happened? This was not his destiny.

Jean turned to her father.

Cotton tossed her the Glock 17.

"Do it," he said.

Jean caught the pistol, perhaps not as gracefully as she might have liked, but then she gripped it hard with both hands and brought the red dot up to the giant cannibal's head. She fought back the tears that wanted to flow from her eyes.

"We're from West Virginia, you son-of-a-bitch," Jean said and pulled the trigger rapidly three times.

The hollow points took apart Barnabas' head, and he fell to the ground.

She stared at his headless body for a moment, and then the tears came. Cotton took her up in his arms.

"It's okay, baby," he whispered as he held her in the darkness.

The Glock 17 fell from her hand and her body shook. Jorge stood off to the side, unsure of what to say or what to do.

In the distance, he saw torches lighting and descending upon the house.

"I know this is bad timing," Jorge said. "But

they're hitting that house and I'd guess everyone is trapped inside. We need to get there now."

Cotton looked up at the man.

"No," he said and stood up. "I've got what I came for. We're leaving."

"What?" Jorge blurted. "I just put my life on the line for you! Roland helped you by sending me and you're just going to walk?"

"That's right," Cotton said.

"We can't," Jean said.

Cotton turned and looked down at her.

"What?" He asked his daughter.

"We can't. April is down there."

"Baby," Cotton said and took a knee. "She's one of them."

"When we found her, I asked you if she was in trouble like Momma was," Jean said. "You told me she was."

Cotton didn't know what to say.

"That man I just killed, he was the enemy," Jean went on. "April isn't. We have to help her. I'm going back to that house."

Cotton looked into her eyes for a moment and for the first time, truly saw the same determination he had always seen in his wife's. He knew his daughter was right.

CHAPTER 11

It was bedlam. Pure, unadulterated chaos. No one was using firearms in the house unless they were at point blank range, and even then, Roland had ordered them to avoid gunfire unless it was absolutely necessary. The last thing they needed was to be accidentally shooting each other. The men were fighting primarily with knives or using their rifles as bludgeoning devices, effectively going hand to hand with the giant cannibals who had stormed the old farmhouse.

Other men were posted at the upstairs windows, shooting down on the advancing horde in an effort to stymie the flow into the structure. It was a plan that could work, it would just be a battle of attrition.

Could they keep up the killing long enough to wipe these animals out and make it out alive?

April picked up two ammunition boxes and ran through the living room, with Brian right behind her. She had already done this twice in the fighting and knew the drill. Don't slow down, don't stop for anything. Just keep going.

She saw one of the Nephilim lunging for her out of the corner of her eye and then he hit the floor. Brian had tackled him and was hammering at his head with the KA-BAR knife he carried. The young man was very winded, but still he kept going. He wrenched his knife free from the Nephilim and caught up with April as she ran up the stairs and quickly deposited the ammo boxes beside the bedroom window.

She then broke one box open with Brian and began loading the empty magazines that littered the floor as Roland held his firing position in the window.

Brian looked April in the eye.

"We're almost out, aren't we?" Brian asked.

April's eyes told him the answer.

She nodded.

Once they had gone through all the ammo, it would be hand-to-hand until the end.

They loaded the last of the magazines and lay them on the floor beside Roland. April slid one into Roland's back pocket.

He turned and gave her a wink.

"Next time you gotta buy me dinner first, darlin'," Roland said.

Despite the intensity and the terror of her current predicament, April couldn't help but smile.

"We're losing the first floor!"

Brian, April, and Roland turned to see Roland's driver Mitchell standing in the doorway. His face was bloody, and he was clearly exhausted.

"What?" Brian asked. He had just been on the lower floor and while it was chaotic, he hadn't seen an indication that they were losing.

"We're being overrun!" Mitchell pressed on. "We need everyone downstairs!"

"Shit!" Roland snapped and pulled his rifle barrel back in the window.

"What?" April asked. "What are we doing?"

Roland looked at her grimly.

"It's called making a final stand."

It was like a scene out of hell as April followed the three men down the stairwell. She had her knife out and could feel tears welling up in her eyes. Her hands were shaking. Was this really how it would end? Several lamps had been lit, but the house was still fairly dark, wild shadows being cast by the flickering lamplight.

She thought that the lighting had been better before she went upstairs.

The Nephilim were finding the lanterns Roland had ordered to be lit and smashing them. They had a lot more experience operating in the dark than Randall and Roland's men did. Their eyes would be more quickly acclimated to fighting in it.

With growing horror, April realized she heard singing. Where was it coming from? Then she understood. The Nephilim were singing "I've found a friend in Jesus."

April's response to this was unexpected, but understandable. It was rage. She had grown up in the church with her father, singing on Sundays and going to Bible study. This was a disgusting perversion of that faith, of her belief. In that moment, she understood that they truly were descending into a man-made hell, to fight for their lives. Perhaps even their very souls.

There was violence at the bottom of the stairs, and she watched Roland, Brian, and Mitchell wade in with their knives, slashing and bludgeoning their way through the crowd. There was no shortage of targets, it was more a problem of differentiating friend from foe.

She hadn't killed anyone up close like this yet, but she knew she wouldn't freeze. Her fear faded away and the only thing left to replace it was cold resolve.

A Nephilim slipped between Roland and Brian and lunged up the stairs for her. His eyes were wild, his bloody teeth smashed out, and his face covered in sweat. April took a hard overhand swing with her knife and buried it in the top of the beast's head, but as he fell, she went with him, her firm grip on the knife handle causing her to be pulled to the floor.

Lying on her side, April wedged her knee into the dead Nephilim's chest and used it as leverage to pull her knife blade from his skull. Just as she freed it, a second tackled her and slammed an elbow into the side of her head.

She felt her skull bounce off the wooden floor, and she blacked out for a split second.

"No!" She screamed and thrust the blade of her knife into the ribs of the cannibal on top of her. She stabbed again and again and again as the Nephilim continued raining blows down on her, then she felt her blade hit something substantial and the blows stopped.

The Nephilim rolled off of her, blood pouring out of his mouth as his body ceased moving. April scrambled to her feet and pushed through the murderous ocean of cannibal warfare, desperate to find a pocket free of the violent frenzy. She could feel that she was running on empty. Killing those two had taken everything she had.

She blinked away the blood in her eyes and then wiped it from her face. She looked down at her hand and saw that it was thick with blood. Her blood or theirs? How badly was she hurt? She tried not to panic as she stumbled into the kitchen.

The kitchen was oddly quiet, the focus of the fighting seeming to be in the rest of the house.

She was leaning back against the sink to catch her breath when she saw them. Three Nephilim turned toward her and entered the kitchen. All three were badly beaten, one with a knife sticking out of his back. They were all wielding hammers and humming the same tune that she had heard the others singing throughout the house.

April propped herself up on the kitchen counter, knees buckling from fatigue. She was desperate to catch her breath.

Then, in a moment, she understood something. She would not die like this. April pushed herself up to a full standing position, leaned forward, and dug her heels in. Her grip tightened on the knife as she brought it up in front of her. She balled up her other fist hard enough that her own fingernails dug into the flesh of her palm. She knew she was trembling and she couldn't stop the tears from flowing, but she wasn't about to give them the satisfaction of cowering.

"Is your soul prepared for judgement?" One of the Nephilim asked as he advanced on her. In the near total darkness, she could barely make them out. Only the moonlight filtering in the kitchen window offered any reprieve from the black.

April said nothing.

"What makes the grass grow?" A voice called out.

April turned. It was coming from inside the wall. It was Jean.

She turned back to the Nephilim and smiled with bloody teeth.

"Blood," she replied to the security challenge.

The pantry door swung open and Cotton Wiley brought up his Glock 17. He fired three shots in rapid succession, killing each Nephilim where they stood.

Jean ran out of the pantry, and April wrapped her arms around the girl. She began breaking down, but Jean leveled her out.

"You're fine," Jean said, wiping some of the blood away from April's face. "You're hurt, but you're not injured. We still have to fight."

"O—Okay," April stammered.

"This place is a freaking shit show," Jorge said as he ducked out of the pantry door behind Cotton. Both men had their night vision devices down and weapons out.

The last of the lanterns had been broken by the Nephilim and the house was now enveloped in total darkness.

"You ready to do some work?" Cotton asked.

"It's been a minute," Jorge replied. "But I think I've still got a few holes left to punch on my dance card."

"Head shots!" April said.

"What?" Cotton asked.

"They have some kind of armor. Take headshots."

"Fantastic," Jorge grumbled. "Giant bulletproof cannibals."

"But they have beautiful singing voices," Cotton replied as the Nephilim continued to sing their hymn.

The two men moved from the kitchen to the living room, slow and short steps, weapons pulled in to the high compress. The first shot Jorge took was placing the muzzle of his Colt directly against the temple of a Nephilim and pulling the trigger.

The flash and sound of the nine-millimeter round was explosive in the dark room and immediately seemed to ratchet the frenzied fighting up to an eleven.

"I'm taking the windows," Cotton said.

Jorge understood. He could see the continual flow of Nephilim entering the house, and plugging those holes was crucial to their gaining control over the structure.

Cotton moved along the perimeter and began taking well-aimed, controlled shots at the big cannibals entering through the smashed-out windows and doors. He could see that even complete sections of wall had been broken out, most likely by the much bigger Nephilim who were carrying sledgehammers.

He felt his slide lock back and, on reflex, his left hand found the magazine on his belt as his right thumb hit the magazine release on the pistol. The empty magazine fell to the floor. He slammed in the fresh one, let the slide go forward and resumed his rate of fire. Normally, he was borderline OCD about never dropping magazines to the ground. He'd always thought it was lazy, but this was not the time to be hunting for a magazine in the darkness.

Outside, he could see that there were still large groups of the advancing Nephilim. In that moment, he saw that just stemming the flow into the house would not be enough. He needed to take the fight to them.

On the floor beside one window, he saw a carbine and snatched it up. It had a good EOTech sight on it and he hit the top side button to switch it to night vision mode. On the floor were a few loaded magazines, which he scooped up as well and stuffed into the pouches on his Haley chest rig.

With the barrel of the carbine, Cotton cleared the rest of the glass out of the window and stepped through it and out onto the ground.

Jorge moved like a buzz saw through the crowd, pistol in one hand and knife in the other. He continued the pattern he had developed of putting his muzzle directly to a Nephilim's head and pulling the trigger. This way he couldn't miss and he also mitigated the possibility of a stray round hitting the wrong person. The trigger pull was often followed by a quick slash with his knife, either killing or seriously wounding his next target. He was setting them up and knocking them down like bowling pins.

He had lost count of how many Nephilim he had killed when he finally slowed down and surveyed the room. They were thinning out.

"Get out of the house!" He shouted. "Now! Get out!"

Cotton moved through the Nephilim, engaging targets of opportunity. He knew he had already killed at least a dozen and also that they somehow still did not realize he was among them. The suppressor on the carbine helped and while it didn't silence the weapon, it made him harder to locate.

He felt the bolt lock back and dropped the magazine from the AR. As this was happening, his left hand pulled the last remaining magazine from his chest rig. It was light. He hadn't noticed this when he picked up the three magazines together inside the house.

There was no other option, so he followed

through with the reload and got back on target. What did the weight of that magazine feel like? Was it ten rounds? Eight? Either way, he'd know in a moment at the rate that he was dropping the giant cannibals.

His eyes were blurring from the repeated action of what amounted to tiny explosions going off next to his face as he fired the carbine. The limited field of view the night vision offered also wasn't helping, effectively locking his nervous system into fight or flight. It had been a long time since he'd been engaged in a full-blown battle like this, and he had forgotten the physical toll it took on him.

Click. That was it. No more rounds for the AR. Cotton dropped the weapon without a second thought and returned to the pistol. He found his dot in the night vision and continued the slaughter. That was the only proper word for what he was doing. Cotton felt nothing as he dropped the Nephilim. They had taken his daughter, tried to kill her. Tried to kill him. A transgression like that could not be allowed to stand.

Click.

The Glock pistol was out of battery, the slide locked back, and no rounds remained. Cotton's left hand dropped to his belt, but he found nothing, as he had already expended those mags. He holstered the

Glock and drew his knife. He looked around. There were still at least two dozen of the Nephilim. He watched them slow the circling action they had been performing around the house and turn toward him. They could barely see him in the quarter moon, but indeed they could now see him.

"Fine," Cotton spat. "Let's go."

Then Cotton watched a wave of men slam into the standing Nephilim, attacking with knives and bare hands. He stepped back and kept his knife up, but understood what was happening. He looked back to the house and could see the remaining fighters exiting the structure. There weren't very many of them, but there were enough.

"Wakey, wakey, eggs and bakey," Roland Reese said as he leaned against the side of the truck.

Cotton opened his eyes and looked up at the sky. He slowly worked himself to an upright position where he had been sleeping in the back of the truck. He couldn't believe how stiff he felt.

"What in the hell?" Cotton muttered.

"You passed out," Roland said, and pointed to Cotton's leg. It was heavily bandaged. "Jorge thinks one of those Nephilim got you good when you were going hand to hand in the tunnels and you just didn't notice it."

"Guess so," Cotton said. He slid out of the back of the truck and stood up, then wobbled for a moment before Roland reached out to steady him. He could feel that the leg was wounded, but it wasn't serious.

"We put an IV in you while you were out," Roland said. "But you still need some solid food. You were also fighting for a long time without a break."

"Mostly fighting your people," Cotton corrected him.

"We'll do the math on that later," Roland said. "But you killed damn near half the residents of central Texas out here."

Cotton turned and looked at the front yard and the old farmhouse. There were bodies everywhere, both Nephilim and Roland's people. One corner of the farmhouse was smoking and several areas on the side of the house had been smashed out.

Jorge stood in the front yard, helping some men stack bodies. They weren't sure yet what they were going to do with all of them, aside from the obvious. Some would become dinner.

Cotton walked to Jorge and extended his hand.

"Good to see you in the light of day," Jorge said

with a smile and shook Cotton's offered hand. "Wasn't sure you were going to make it there."

"Been through worse," Cotton said. "But not much."

Jorge looked around.

"Yeah, me too."

"Hey," Cotton said. "Thank you. Sincerely. I couldn't have gotten her back without you. I know that."

"We all need help out here," Jorge said. "I think I kind of figured that out last night too."

"Daddy!"

Cotton turned and saw Jean running toward him. He also became acutely aware for the first time that she was the only human among a group of cannibals. He remembered something he had heard at the beginning of everything. Cannibals would eat each other, but comparing the taste of a cannibal to the taste of a human was like comparing a day-old McDonald's hamburger to a filet mignon right off the grill. He made a mental note to never forget that.

"Baby Bear!" Cotton said and gathered her up in his arms. He held her for a moment before pushing back her hair and checking her for injuries.

"I'm fine," Jean said. "Couple scrapes and bruises but I'm not hurt."

Cotton let out a breath.

"It's okay," Jean said. "We're going to be okay."

Cotton looked up from where he was crouching beside Jean and stood up.

April looked like she had been through a war, because she had. Her left eye was swollen shut and her lip was split. Various other cuts and bruises peppered her face as well as her arms and hands.

"Jesus," Cotton gasped. "Are you okay?"

April managed a weak smile.

"Funny thing is, I feel better than I have in a long time."

"You did good," Cotton said.

"She did great," Roland corrected him. He put his hand on April's shoulder. "This girl's a freaking pipe hitter."

April's smile got a little bigger and Cotton noted the look the two shared. Was something going on there?

Randall Eisler walked across the front yard and joined the small group that was forming.

Roland held his gaze for a moment. He knew what he had to ask, but didn't want to get the answer.

"How many left?" Roland asked.

Randall Eisler looked around the yard and then back to Roland.

"Only folks that came with you and survived is Jorge, Mitchell and that Brian kid. I've got six left. That leaves us with eleven total."

"What was the total in the beginning?" Cotton asked.

"About seventy," Randall Eisler said grimly. "I do reckon you would have got your ass beat."

Cotton smiled.

"Glad it didn't go that way," Cotton said.

"Wait a minute," Roland said. "What about Harris and his men?"

Randall set his jaw.

"Funny thing about that," Randall Eisler said. "They ain't nowhere to be found."

"Their bodies?" Roland asked.

"No," Randall Eisler said. "They ain't nowhere. As in, I think they ran."

Roland considered this for a moment and then nodded.

"We will attend to that matter after we get ourselves organized. There ain't many places they can run where I can't find them," Roland said, then turned to Cotton. "What do you do now?"

"Same as before," Cotton said.

"Alaska?" Roland asked. "After what I told you? You still want to go through that mess?"

"No choice," Cotton replied. "Hell, we were only here for less than a day and look what happened. I just need a place to lay my head that has fewer people."

"Go where people aren't," Roland repeated what he had said earlier.

"That's right."

Roland looked at his old friend for a moment and then nodded his head.

"Okay, I get it, but let me get you outfitted. You saved our assess at the end there, I don't think anyone can question that." Roland looked around and saw no dissenting looks, even if they would not offer their gratitude out loud. "You don't have to stay; we don't have to go to senior prom together. Just let me get you set up with a vehicle, some food and whatever else you need. Maybe along the way you find out a little more about what we're doing, but the choice is still yours."

Cotton's gut was screaming not to take the offer, but he couldn't just ignore the fact that they were bare bones. He could probably find most of their supplies in the carnage of the farmhouse, but even that hadn't been much. He'd also known Roland Reese for damn near twenty years. Did that kind of loyalty go away just because someone was a little less human?

"All right," Cotton said. "If you can help us get set up, I'm not going to turn you down, but believe me when I tell you that nothing I see is going to change my mind."

"Understood," Roland replied, but there was something about him that said he may have understood, but he did not agree.

"Jorge, can you take Jean through the house to collect what she can find of our things?" Cotton asked.

"Will do," Jorge replied.

Cotton turned to April.

"Can I talk to you?"

"Sure," April replied slowly, and followed him to the edge of the yard.

Cotton turned for a moment and watched the men loading up the vehicles, then turned back to April.

"Is there something going on?" Cotton asked. "Between you and Roland?"

April looked embarrassed, and Cotton knew the answer.

"Come on," April said. "I've known him for like five minutes."

"Well, I've known him for like twenty years. He's got the Kavorka."

"The what?" April asked.

"Didn't you ever watch Seinfeld?"

"I was more of a 'Friends' girl," April responded.

"You are now dead to me," Cotton said. "Anyway, he's got this thing. Women are drawn to him."

"I look like I just went a hundred rounds with Mike Tyson," April said. "I don't think he's interested."

"Sure," Cotton smirked. "Either way, you'll need to decide where you're going soon."

"What do you mean?"

"Well, I'm sure you'll have an open invitation from Roland," Cotton said. "I'm also sure that guy over there who kidnapped you, infected you with the vaccine and then used you as bait, would be happy to take you in."

"Fat fucking chance of that happening," April said, and then thought about it. "Are you saying that going with you might be an option?"

"Well, I figure we already taught you about toilet paper tablets and where the trigger is on an AR—"

"I told you that in confidence!"

"Either way, it would be kind of a waste to lose you now. You don't have to go the distance with us, but maybe you can figure out where you belong along the way."

"Okay," April said.

"Okay what?" Cotton asked.

"Okay, I'm going with you."

"Good," Cotton said, maintaining his stoicism. "But I think we should keep this between us. At least for now."

"Okay, we're pretty sure the Nephilim are all dead, but not one hundred percent sure. Knowing that, I think we need to stick together for now," Roland said as he stood in front of the Mercedes SUV. All those assembled nodded their heads. "Good. Considering that, we'll head to Oatmeal first to get re-outfitted and do a thorough damage assessment."

"Can't do that," Randall Eisler said. "I need to check in on my people. They took the vaccine yesterday and I need to know how they're doing."

"Use the radio," Roland said.

"Ain't workin'," Randall Eisler replied. "Been trying to raise 'em the last couple hours and get nothing."

"No sat phone?" Roland asked.

"We're simple folk," Randall Eisler said. "Only got the two sat phones. One went with Jorge and the other's in my truck."

Roland stared hard at Randall Eisler for a moment and then shook his head.

"I don't like this," Roland said.

Randall Eisler walked to the King of Texas and lowered his voice.

"Look, I have to check on my people. You understand. If I have to do it alone, that's fine, but that leaves you with no one. You run into trouble on your way to Oatmeal, and well... I guess we both know how that story probably ends."

This felt distinctly like a threat.

"You better think real careful about where you're going with this line of thinking," Roland said firmly.

"It ain't a threat," Randall Eisler said. "It's just the way it is. I think you know that."

"But I don't have to like it."

"Fair enough."

Roland thought about this. He turned to Mitchell.

"How was the check in?" Roland asked.

"All good," Mitchell said and held up the sat

phone. "Getting a little interference on the net from something, but otherwise they said it was all quiet."

Roland looked at his watch and sighed. He knew Randall Eisler was right, but either way, this was going to screw up his whole timeline.

"Shit!" He spat and then turned back to Mitchell. "Call them back. Relay a message to Sheila to start dispensing the vaccine."

This caught Jorge's attention.

Jesus, Jorge thought. *She's really going to do it. She's going to take the vaccine. Should I be taking it? Would that change anything between us?*

"Okay," Roland said. "We're going to Cypress Mill. We'll check on Randall Eisler's people and then from there we'll move on to Oatmeal, unless anyone's got any fucking opinions to the contrary?"

Roland wasn't really asking for input, that much was clear. He had reached his limit with suggestions from the foot soldiers.

Cotton stood at the edge of the yard, surveying the scores of the dead. He looked down at his hands for a moment. He felt good. Maybe it was just the adrenaline, but it might also be that he missed this. He missed the fight. Running wasn't in his nature, but that was all he seemed to do lately.

He looked over his shoulder and saw Jorge and Jean walking toward him. Jorge had Cotton's ruck sack and Jean had her smaller pack, as well as her MK18 carbine and her Glock 19 in its holster.

"Get everything?" Cotton asked.

"Everything we can carry," Jean confirmed.

Cotton looked across the yard to where everyone was loading up vehicles.

"Why don't you take it on over to Jorge's truck and get ready to go?"

Jean nodded and walked away.

Cotton watched her.

"She's a good girl," Jorge said. "Smart and tough."

"She gets that from her mother."

"So did mine," Jorge said.

Cotton didn't ask.

"You were Delta?" Cotton asked.

"We never say the 'D-Word,'" Jorge replied with a smile. "But, yeah. I was with the Unit for almost eight years. Mostly in Iraq but a couple of tours in Afghanistan."

"You got lucky," Cotton said. "Afghanistan sucked."

Jorge laughed.

"Roland said you were with him at Development Group."

"That was a long time ago," Cotton said.

Jorge studied the man for a moment. There was clearly something off about him. His eyes blinked rapidly as he talked and he seemed at times to be unsteady on his feet, but Jorge understood how those problems worked. When the rounds started flying, Cotton Wiley would be just fine. It was like how Ozzy Osbourne used to look like a ninety-year-old man on camera when he was being interviewed, but then he'd get on stage and be doing back flips.

"You can trust me," Jorge said. "I know those are just words right now, but you can."

Cotton nodded.

"What's the dumbest thing you ever did?" Cotton asked.

"What?"

"On a real-world op," Cotton said. "What was the dumbest thing you ever did?"

Jorge smiled.

"I zip tied my tourniquet to my gear."

"What?" Cotton asked. "Why in the hell would you do that?"

"Everyone was rubber banding them to their

plate carriers," Jorge said with a shrug. "I thought a zip tie would be even more secure."

"So secure, you can't ever get it off."

Jorge laughed.

"What about you? What's the dumbest thing you ever did?"

Cotton looked around at the men loading up the trucks preparing for the journey west to Cypress Mill.

"This," Cotton said. "This is the dumbest thing I've ever done."

Jorge smiled and turned to see Roland Reese waving him over to where he stood beside the Mercedes SUV.

"Looks like I'm being summoned by his majesty," Jorge said. He could see that there was something else on Cotton's mind. "What is it?"

"Look.... It ain't my place to say, but I've known Roland a long time."

"That's what I hear," Jorge said.

"We spent a lot of time together, and I love him like a brother."

"I feel like there's a 'but' coming," Jorge surmised.

"Don't trust him," Cotton said, his face becoming

deadly serious. "He wants to win. It's all he cares about."

Jorge nodded his understanding.

"Closing business?" Jorge asked as he approached Roland.

Roland looked around and then back to the big man.

"I need you to go to Tow for me."

"Tow?" Jorge asked, clearly caught off guard. "Why do you need me to go all the way out there?"

"You know those hippies have been camped out for a while doing their whole 'Gatherer' thing. Well, I've got a deal in place with them and so I've got a vested interest in doing what I can to keep them breathing. Something tells me this thing ain't over."

"I get the same sense," Jorge agreed. "What kind of deal you got with them?"

Roland hesitated.

"I'm off the hook, right?" Jorge asked. "That was the deal when we left Oatmeal. So, now you're asking for extra credit. Think I deserve to know why."

"Okay," Roland said. "They've got a guy there that can build radios and repair sat phones. He's been keeping us up and running this whole time. He can fix weapons too. We've been at this for a while, going on two years now. Gear's getting old. We need to make sure we've got people who can fix it."

"Makes sense," Jorge said.

"And I figure they'll come into the fold eventually. This Gatherer shit can't last forever."

Jorge turned to look at Cotton and then back to Roland.

"What's the deal with him?" Jorge asked. "You really gonna let him walk?"

"I really am," Roland said. "That there is one man I have no interest in going to war against."

"Why is that?" Jorge asked. "What makes him so special?"

"It's hard to put a pin in it," Roland said. "He's just different. I've seen him do things in training and in combat that just can't be explained. I literally watched him walk out of a burning building once in Iraq. Fire didn't touch him. I know he's got some Shawnee Indian in him, maybe that has something to do with it. Crazy thing about it is... he didn't seem to notice. His eyes were somewhere else. He just walked up to me and said it was time to flex to the next target."

"Okay," Jorge said with a nod. "I'll go to Tow for you. I'll take the kid Brian with me."

"Thank you," Roland said. "Like I told you back in Oatmeal, I ain't forgotten what you did for me."

"At least it meant something, putting it on you," Jorge said.

Roland smiled and looked around.

"Wonder how much it would change things?" Roland asked. "If they all knew you were the one who really killed the President?"

Six Hours Earlier...

June Kennedy stood in the living room of the small two-bedroom house and watched the dawn break outside her window. It was beautiful. It was beautiful in a way that she had never noticed before the destruction of the world as she knew it. Like so many people, she had been caught up in the day-to-day trivialities of work, social media, raising children and walking on the hamster wheel that would one day end with her unceremonious death.

Then it all went away. That was when the little things mattered so much more. That was when she began noticing how sweet each breath smelled, how good food tasted and, yes, how beautiful each sunrise was.

For a fleeting moment, she wondered if that had anything to do with having turned, having become what she now was. People talked about that possibility. They knew that once people became cannibals (because that is what they were; she had to keep reminding herself), they were stronger, faster and seemingly free of any disease. Were all the senses heightened as well?

If this second generation of the vaccine worked the way it was supposed to, the way they promised it would, she would know soon enough.

What if she turned back, and the world became a mere shadow of itself? What if the cancer came back? Without the hyper-immunity granted by the first vaccine, would it return?

She was willing to risk it. In truth, it had never even been a question. She was being given the opportunity to regain her humanity, to no longer be a monster.

June walked into the bathroom and looked at her reflection in the mirror over the sink.

She contemplated her own milky white eyes.

That was what she was. A monster. She ate other

humans to survive. She was the thing that went bump in the night.

She looked at the clock on the wall. It had been fourteen hours since she took the vaccine. Shouldn't something have happened by now? Some kind of change?

She leaned into the mirror and inspected her eyes. It had been an assumption that if the vaccine caused you to regain your humanity, the pigment in your eyes should come back as well. What if it didn't?

June thought back to the Processing House and the Slaughterhouse Five. She had hated that place, hated those men. She understood they had to eat, but not like that. Those men took pleasure in what they did. Was she any better, though? Was she any less of a monster? She had thought that by working with Randall Eisler to organize the community, she could somehow tamp down the brutality, but she had been lying to herself. It was about her own survival. Nothing more.

She stared into her own dead eyes and watched the tears forming.

What if it didn't work? Should she just end it? Be done with it?

"You motherfucker," she sobbed as she stared at

the monster looking back at her. She shouted, "Monster!"

June slammed her hand down against the edge of the sink and watched it shatter.

Her sobbing ceased. She stepped back and looked at what she had done. She grabbed what remained of the sink and ripped it from the wall. In her shock, she dropped it to the ground. She could feel something building inside of her, some kind of rage that was becoming harder to suppress.

June Kennedy turned and slammed her fist into the wall, but instead of striking the wall, her hand went through the drywall and broke the stud within. She threw a half dozen more blows with the same effect before turning back to the mirror.

Her eyes had gone black. Twin orbs of coal that stared back at her. Her body was different as well. The veins in her arms stood out in bold relief and her skin had a more intense pink hue to it. She looked closely and saw that steam was rising from her body. Very subtle, but it was there. Her skin was hot. She put her hand to her forehead and could feel that she was burning up.

June could feel her anger continuing to rise until she bared her teeth and wanted to scream. There was a frenzy inside of her, voices in her head telling her she was starving. She gripped the mirror of the medicine cabinet and tore it off, then threw it across the room as she screamed.

She turned back and saw the bottle. It had been so long since she needed it. She picked up the orange prescription bottle of Thorazine, popped the cap off, fished out a pill and chewed it furiously. Her hands were trembling.

The frenzy was building. She could feel her body shaking. Her muscles were contracting so hard that she feared they may break her bones.

She took out another pill, crushed it in her hand, and quickly snorted it. She had seen in some movie that this could get medication into your system faster. It was probably bullshit. Most things in movies were.

June fell to the floor and pulled her body into the fetal position. She could feel the tension in every joint. Her heart was beating out of her chest.

"Please!" She whimpered. "Just let me die."

Then everything went quiet. Her heart slowed down, the frenzy reduced to a rolling boil within her and her muscles relaxed.

June held out her hands and looked at them. They were covered in blood.

"What?" She whispered to herself.

She could feel that she was exhausted, but she dragged herself to her feet. She looked down at her reflection in one of the shards of broken mirror on the floor and saw she was covered in blood. She had been under such intense physiological stress that she had begun sweating blood.

There was a knock at the door.

June let out a breath and turned to the living room.

"June?" A voice called out. It was her neighbor, Mike Sanford. "Is everything okay? I heard noises."

June walked across the cool tile floor of the bathroom and then onto the hardwood floor of the living room. Something was different. She could feel more. Her body felt electric.

She stopped at the living room door and opened it.

Mike stood there, his eyes wide as he faced the woman with black eyes covered in blood.

"June?" He asked, confused.

They had been friends since she came to the community. One could even say they were good friends. They'd had dinner many times and as Mike missed his wife (who had gone to live in a city) terribly, there was never any of the awkwardness that often came along with friendships between men and women.

"Did you take it?" June asked, cocking her head to the side.

"Take it?" Mike asked.

"The new vaccine," June clarified.

"No."

June slammed her fist through the front of Mike's head and it exited the back of his skull. She opened her hand and felt a few involuntary twitches before his body went limp, hanging on her forearm. She withdrew her hand with lightning speed and let him fall to the ground.

In short order, she separated his head from the rest of his body and did what her nature demanded of her. She consumed him, but only what lay above the shoulders. In a moment of clarity, she understood that the meat of the body was for the dogs, not for her. She was more evolved than that.

The screams were beginning. She looked up from her crouched position and watched three of the unevolved dogs overtake a man in the street. They were instantly on him, taking him apart and feeding. One of them turned to her. She was different. He could see this. He fixed his black eyes on hers and moved toward her, blood and saliva dripping from his lips, his movements wild and jerky.

"No!" June said and snapped her fingers. She stood up and pointed a long, blood and gore covered finger at him. "You know who I am!"

The man stopped in his tracks. He was still clearly in a frenzy, but there was also an understanding. He did know who she was. He held her gaze for a moment and then turned and ran down the street, onto the next meal.

They were sharks now. No more building societies, no pretending to still be human. They would only hunt, and when there was no one left to hunt, they would simply die.

Frank opened his third Coca-Cola of the night and sat back in his chair. It wasn't really night anymore. Dawn had just broken. His shift was almost over. He looked at the can of coke and wondered why he still drank them. He couldn't taste the soda; it was just like bubbly water. Except that even water had more of a taste than this. Like Randall Eisler had said, it was mostly about the habit. For a moment, he wondered how many cans were left in the storehouse. Perhaps he should dial back this habit, because while he couldn't taste them, the sugary drinks most likely weren't doing his teeth any favors.

He looked at his watch. It was nearly eight in the morning. Where in the hell was his relief? They were supposed to start the change of guard at fifteen minutes till, not right on the damn hour.

Frank was not pleased when Randall Eisler asked him to stay behind and secure the community. He thought that was a lot of bullshit. After all, he was one of the few people in the town who actually had military experience.

As it turned out that was a big part of why Randall Eisler wanted him to stay behind. This whole trip out to that house to root out one guy was likely going to be a giant nothing burger. Keeping the town secure was a different matter. That was actually important. They needed a man like Frank to be on point for that.

Frank mused on this as he sat at the communications desk monitoring the HAM radio net. Despite being the so-called 'outcasts' of modern American society, the City States still relied upon the news they received from outposts like Cypress Mill. In exchange for daily status reports, the outposts would receive news in return, as well as the occasional supply drop. It was a strange agreement, but one that (at least for the time being) seemed necessary.

This was how they had received a batch of the Gen 2 Vaccine. Frank wasn't sure what he thought about that. He understood that some folks had a desire to regain what they thought of as their 'humanity', but Frank was not one of them. He liked being a cannibal. Not only that, but he considered himself to have become quite a skilled hunter of men.

If he was being honest about it, he even kind of enjoyed it. Sort of in the same way those misfits the Slaughterhouse Five did.

Outside his window, Frank saw a man running down the main street being pursued by several other men.

"What in the hell?" Frank muttered as he leaned forward in his chair and peered outside. "Must have been caught stealing."

The radio on the desk crackled to life, and Frank snatched up the microphone. That was strange. The situation report wasn't scheduled to go out until noon.

"Calling all stations, this is Houston Station," a voice crackled across the frequency.

"Houston Station, this is Cypress Mill," Frank

replied.

"Thank God," the voice came back. "What's your status?"

"Status?" Frank asked, confused. "I don't know. Normal."

"Did you take the vaccine yet?"

"No," Frank replied. "Well, I mean, I didn't, but the others did."

"Get out now!" The voice implored. "Our citizens began the protocol yesterday at noon and we lost control in the last hour."

"Lost control?" Frank asked. "What are you talking about?"

"Houston has fallen!" The voice said.

"The— The whole city?" Frank stammered.

"Yes! They're tearing people apart!"

There was a cacophony of noises coming from the background of the transmission, shouts, and banging sounds. There was also something that sounded like growling.

"Hey, what's going on out there?" Frank asked.

"They're— They're trying to get inside," the voice said and began degenerating into crying. "Please, I'm so scared. I want my mom."

"What?" Frank asked.

He knew it was a grown man he was talking to and not some child.

"I have to find someplace. I have to find someplace else to hide," the man whimpered.

The line went dead.

Frank was frozen. He felt as if the man's fear was contagious. There were nearly a million people in Houston. It was one of the largest City States. What did he mean it had "fallen?"

Frank looked up and saw June Kennedy standing in the doorway.

"June!" He exclaimed, then stopped. "What happened to you?"

Right away, he could see that she was covered in blood, but then he saw her eyes, her coal-black eyes.

June stepped forward, and Frank saw she was holding a long-handled axe by her side, dragging the blade along the floor.

"I always wondered what all those Bible thumpers were talking about when they said they'd been born again," June said. "Now I know."

Without warning, she swung the axe forward and buried the blade in the side of Frank's neck. He scrambled, grabbing furiously at the handle, but he was no match for June as she used the axe to push him out of his chair and into the wall. She jammed her foot into his torso to free the axe and then swung it repeatedly into him until his body was no longer recognizable as having once been a man.

Once this work was done, she discarded the axe, broke his head open and consumed what had once made him who he was.

As June knelt on the floor, she could feel the power building within her, and she could hear the collective voice of the Evolved swirling in her consciousness. They were one, but they were a storm without direction. Starving and insane.

She would be the one to give them direction.

She stood back up and pulled the bottle of Thorazine from the pocket of her blood-stained summer dress. She shook it and smiled. They were the only reason she wasn't just another of those hungry dogs rampaging through the streets. That was the only plausible explanation.

June stepped to the door and saw another pack of them running down Main Street. She put her fingers to her lips and let out a sharp whistle.

The pack slowed down and turned to her. They were like she was, at least in appearance. Black eyes, steam coming off their bodies, bulging veins and bright pink skin.

"Come here," June called out.

The pack moved to her and stood in silence.

"You listen to me, don't you?" June asked.

They said nothing.

"Hm," she said. "I wonder if you all do? I wonder if, perhaps... I have an army now?"

June walked back into the comms center, picked up the microphone, and hit the call button.

"Calling all stations on the net," June said softly as she held the microphone and looked out the window at the chaos devouring the community. "Cypress Mill has fallen."

**The story continues in
Cannibal Warfare Book Two: Survival Of
The Sickest**

**If you enjoyed this book please consider
providing a review on Amazon.**

ABOUT THE AUTHOR

 **Jordan Vezina** is a fiction writer living in Austin, Texas with his wife Emily where they run a business together. Jordan served in both the Marine Corps and Army Infantry, and worked as a bodyguard. This background provided much of the detail regarding weapons and tactics in Jordan's books.

Make sure to sign up at Jordanvezina.com to get three free books, including one not available on Amazon.

jordanvezina.com
hello@jordanvezina.com

Printed in Great Britain
by Amazon

82718853R00183